Undercover: Crime Sh

Jane Risdon

What My Readers Say:

Undercover – Crime Shorts; is a wonderfully satisfying anthology of seven short stories which transcend above the crime fiction genre providing a ripping yarn irrespective of the reader's crime fiction preference. Jane Risdon has cleverly stitched together a mix of tales to suit all fans of the genre. Roger A. Price former detective and author of *Nemesis and Vengeance.*

Jane Risdon is an author of exceptional talent. When you get the opportunity to read her work you certainly should, she is an awesome talent. She gives a view in her writing which is both full of imagination and technique. An author who knows exactly how to convey her thoughts and ideas to her readers and her writing is of a calibre and quality only seen in the very best authors. Jeff Lee author of *Chump Change, The Ladies Temperance Club's Farewell Tour and Scrotus.*

Tina Jaray, Reader.
Wow, I could hardly breathe while I read this. Glad it was short or I would've joined the corpse!

Gloria Clulow, Reader.
As with all your stories I find them intriguing and unpredictable, leaving me wanting more; I don't want them to end.

Murder by Christmas: Murder by Christmas is a brilliant read. The author displays excellent skills as she tells the story from several perspectives, all of which help keep the twists and turns a surprise. Thoroughly recommended. Roger A. Price former detective and author of *Nemesis and Vengeance*

Murder by Christmas: What a fantastic story. I was glued to the screen and stopped work which means another late night (thanks). Dave Michael Prosser, *Author of the Barsetshire Diaries and more.*

The Honey Trap: Great Story. You completely blind-sided me with your twist at the end. I didn't see that one coming. Loved it. Jane is an awesome writer and an author of exceptional talent. Jeff Lee author of *Chump Change, The Ladies Temperance Club's Farewell Tour and Scrotus.*

Undercover: What a gripping story, so well written. You've packed so much 'punch' into it, loved it. I really felt the rising tension and suspicion! You've captured the suspense of it beautifully and it is such a great set-up with good characters. Margot Kinberg *Associate Professor and author of the Joel Williams novels.*

Undercover: Wow, Jane, this is one of the best stories I've ever read! It doesn't matter that it's so short, I was right there with her and this blew me away. You are such a good writer! Stacy Margaret Allan, *Author of Sorrow Dreams*

About the Author

Jane Risdon writes crime thrillers often set in the music business or with an organised crime or espionage element. With a former career in the international music business managing songwriters, singers, musicians, and record producers, she often draws upon her experiences in Hollywood, Europe and SE Asia for her plots.

She is also the author of a variety of short stories which have been included in 15 anthologies to date, as well as in online magazines and newsletters where she also contributes articles and flash fiction stories. Two of the anthologies she has contributed towards are *award winners.*

Jane has co-authored the award-winning Only One Woman (Accent Press Ltd) with long-time friend and best-selling, award-winning author, Christina Jones, which is a love triangle set in the UK music scene of the late 1960s. Jane is married to a musician and has drawn upon her knowledge and experiences of her life in the music business for her first outing into Women's Fiction. Only One Woman was published in paperback 24th May 2018 and is also available in Waterstones and on most digital platforms internationally.

Undercover: Crime Shorts - a collection bringing some of her short stories together for the first time. If you enjoy a gripping yarn with more twists and turns than Spaghetti Junction, you should enjoy this collection. There's another collection to follow soon.

Follow her on:

Facebook: https://www.facebook.com/JaneRisdon2/
Amazon Author Page: https://www.amazon.co.uk/-/e/B00I3GJ2Y8
Author Blog: https://janerisdon.wordpress.com/
Jane on Accent Press: https://accentpressbooks.com/collections/jane-risdon
Twitter: https://twitter.com/Jane_Risdon
Instagram: https://www.instagram.com/janerisdonwriter/

Jane loves to hear from readers and is happy to receive their comments.

Dedication

This collection is dedicated to my soul-mate who has had to read everything I have ever written and still smiles with delight afterwards. It is also dedicated to all the wonderful readers and authors who have supported me on my writing journey – thanks one and all. You rock. Jane Risdon

Contents:

SWEET SABLE - The Red Siren

Chapter One

Closing the safe door quietly and with an expert spin of the dial the black-clad woman straightened up, slinging the grip with her haul over her shoulder. She stood listening intently before moving towards the office door. Again she waited, her ears straining, before gently prising the door open and stepping silently into the corridor of darkened offices. She eased the door closed calculating she had barely two minutes before the night-watchman made his rounds, trying the doors and checking the building was secure.

The woman headed for the fire escape where she'd made her entrance to the three storey building some ten minutes earlier. Gently raising the window she climbed out on to the metal staircase with the athletic grace of a ballet dancer, giving the dark alley below a quick once-over to ensure no-one was around she hastily made her way down the rusting stairs. Her tar- toned unremarkable and unmemorable automobile was parked across the street, hidden in the gloom of another narrow alleyway. Glancing at her wrist-watch – an expensive pay-off from a married lover - she knew she'd better step on the gas. She'd less than fifteen minutes to get back to the night-club, park her car at the darkest end of the outside lot, and leg it back to her dressing-room with enough time to change into her gown for her last set of the evening.

The red-head chuckled to herself as she repaired her lipstick pouting seductively at herself in the mirror, waiting for the stagehand to knock on her door with her final call. She was buzzing. She'd done it again, she'd pulled it off. It was better than any sex she'd ever had and that was saying something. She chuckled, puckered her ample lips and blew herself a huge wet kiss.

*****

As the spotlight found its mark the band-leader nodded to the scarlet-clad shapely figure who took up position in front of the microphone. Her hips swayed in time to the jazz trumpet and she took her cue. Her sultry sable-clad tones sucked her audience into her lair.

The figures outlined in the flickering candle-light adorning circular tables dotted around the smoke-hazed, expectant venue, stopped talking and turned their heads towards the elevated stage where Desi Garcia's

1

Syncopators went into full swing behind Sweet Sable - also known as the Red Siren – neither was her real name but no-one cared. When her song ended there was a moment's silence before they pounded their tables shouting, 'more, more.'

Sweet Sable wiggled her slender but shapely hips, leaned over the stage giving more than an eye-full of her full bosom on display in her tight-fitting, strapless gown and blew huge smackers into the air, aimed at no-one in particular but the full-blooded men in the audience got the message and so did their partners who silently seethed.

Her set over for the evening Sweet Sable made her way back to her dressing room, accepting compliments and congratulations on her 'wonderful performance,' smiling, blowing kisses and with a toss of her luxurious red mane, closed her dressing room door to keep the *stage door Johnnies* out. There was always a small stud congregated outside her door and gathered around the stage door following her shows. Sometimes she allowed a particularly handsome or obviously loaded guy inside who was good for a dinner or two - or for something else - if rich enough. They were ripe for the picking; such *patsies*.

This particular evening Sweet Sable was anxious not to have any company. She had plans and getting pawed by a fawning, slobbering man who felt 'entitled' after giving her dinner, was not part of them. She had to get her haul to a safe place so she could take a proper look at it before deciding what she had to do. Sweet Sable loved having options – and she had plenty.

Chapter Two

An hour later a blonde haired Sweet Sable sipped her Knickerbocker cocktail slowly as she looked through her ill-gotten gains. She was sitting in the darkest lit booth of her favourite gin joint - a little bar just off Wiltshire Boulevard. She'd been a regular on and off for years and they left her to her own devices. She never had anyone with her when she dropped in, she kept to herself and always drank the same cocktail. No-one ever got 'conversational' or asked questions; it wasn't the type of joint where it would've been appreciated. The drinkers frequenting Gino's weren't the forgiving type, the bartenders didn't want to risk what might happen should they get too curious or friendly. Sweet Sable was confident that she - and what she was looking at - was invisible as far as the other occupants were concerned; as they were to her.

There were the typical items she'd found in many of the safes she'd cracked over the years: Wills, Share Certificates, Deeds and such like – lots of bundles of the green stuff, which would be untraceable and very handy – but no love letters - pity, they were always a good earner. She counted over three thousand dollars. Very nice, she thought. A small pouch revealed twenty small diamonds which took her breath away. She looked up ensuring no-one was curious about the platinum blonde and what she was looking at. Nobody seemed overly interested in her. She put the diamonds back in the velvet pouch – she had just the fence for them.

She took a long satisfied sip of her cocktail and turned her attention to the purpose of her raid on the offices of her former lover, Jack Grady: loving father to two teenage girls, devoted husband of the wealthy socialite, Jennifer Getty, and a sheep in wolf's clothing as far as Sweet Sable was concerned. Jack was also a successful business-man and someone who had his sticky fingers in many pies. He was as rotten as week-old meat left out for the trash which attracted coyotes from the canyons on the edge of Hollywood. Hollywood was full of coyotes and not all walked on four legs, Sweet Sable thought. He'd fit right in to City Hall, she mused, thinking of his political ambitions.

Jack, what a mistake he made. He'd come to her dressing room after a performance six months ago. Handsome, suave, and oozing sex-appeal and, more importantly, he had money. She was smitten first sight – as far as she'd ever allow herself to be - and the fact he was loaded made him even more attractive. He was ripe for a good time and so was she. Sweet Sable had him eating out of her hand within days and soon it was clear he was addicted. She played him, strung him along, getting what she could out of him before she'd give him the inevitable brush off.

He'd lavished gifts upon her, paid her rent for her new apartment and he'd even given her a new auto – nothing too flashy, attracting unwanted attention, of course, she'd seen to that. He'd given her diamonds, gold, jewellery, and paid for expensive clothes. Jack was generous to a fault. She'd got a meal ticket for a while at least. It had all been so easy, she'd even thought about giving up singing and just doing the odd 'job' when the *rush* needed topping up. It was tempting to take it all for granted.

But he'd started to cool off. She was getting the flick, the brush-off, he didn't take her calls and was vague about arranging dates. Well, she hadn't come down in the last shower – he'd picked the wrong one this time. No-one did that to her. The younger dame from his office had succeeded with her tight-fitting suits, fluttering lashes and *little girl lost* act in polishing his ego and now he wanted to set her up. He wanted Sable to find a new apartment, without his patronage.

Sweet Sable wasn't going to hit her head against his walnut dashboard - she was pragmatic - but she was also unforgiving. Jack didn't know what she was capable of, who she was – what she was. Now she had something he'd pay for, something he'd beg her for! No-one gave Sweet Sable the elbow. Even if she didn't care two hoots about who was giving it.

Chapter Three

Benny *the fence* handed over the money for the diamonds, no questions asked. He didn't know her name, didn't want to. The sulky blonde had been using him for years and so far things had worked just fine. They spoke little. She always wore huge dark glasses, a dark overcoat with the collar turned up over her face covering her features. In moments she was gone. Picking her out in a line-up would've been impossible. He had protection so she wasn't a threat to him. She knew it too. They both did.

Sweet Sable replaced the floorboard in her bedroom over her money and *'insurance,'* with the rug and couch covering it, she poured a bourbon and settled cross-legged on the couch. She almost had enough put aside to disappear forever, to begin a new life anywhere she wanted - Rio perhaps. But the men there were rich and might prove too tempting in her retirement, so perhaps not. Once she'd dealt with Jack she'd decide. The diamond haul gave her a small fortune by anyone's thinking - but her other finds, well, there was a huge fortune to be made if she played it right.

She sipped her drink thinking about all the guys she'd seen off over the last ten years. She got one hell of a kick from it but she was also getting weary. The rush wasn't quite the same any more. Sometimes it was too easy somehow, too much of a walkover. The redhead loved a challenge, the seduction, the chase, and then the kill. How Sweet Sable loved the kill.

Jack Grady led a double life too. He had secrets his now former lover knew he had. You get that rich and that successful, you just had to have skeletons; now she knew where his were hidden. She leaned back against the leather couch and smiled, a slow, sly smile. Time to rattle Jack's bones. 'Cheers Jack,' she lifted her glass and winked into space.

*****

Her phone rang before the birds were up. Sweet Sable struggled to clear her mind of the fog which descended every time she popped the knock-out pills. 'Yeah,' she coughed and peered at the clock beside her bed. You gotta be kidding, she thought.

'You got something belonging to a mutual friend who wants it back.'

'What?' she sat up slowly, her mind clearing fast, 'who is this?' Few people had her number and she didn't recognise the rasping voice; Italian, male, she decided.

'Look lady I'm not making a social call, cut the crap. Who I am don't matter. You listen to me good coz I ain't repeating myself.' The voice waited. Sable tried to think.

'You gone deaf or what? Say something,' he said, a little louder.

'I dunno what you mean, who is this?' she played dumb as she got out of bed and tried to get her robe on singlehandedly. She went to the window and eased the blind up a little, her bleary eyes trawling the street. Nothing.

'You don't want to mess with me lady, stop playing dumb, we both know you ain't.' Sable could hear the man draw on a cigarette, then cough. 'You got something don't belong to you and you're gonna give it to me.'

'I dunno you, take a hike,' she said, and slammed the phone down pulling the lead from the wall, her heart beating so fast she couldn't hear anything else. Change of plan - for now.

It took her about thirty minutes to get her stuff together, get her stash from under the floorboard and leave her apartment. She was used to hasty exits and always paid her rent in advance just in case she had to do a moonlight. Jack had always been generous and she had saved. Her pay from the nightclub was cash in hand on the night so they didn't owe her. They'd find another singer soon enough. Hollywood was crawling with them

Chapter Four

Keeping her eye on the road behind her she drove her latest new car out of town heading towards Big Bear Mountain where she had a secret hideaway, a secure log cabin which she used whenever the going got too hot. It was isolated - although not far from the main lake - hidden from anyone out in a boat and from casual walkers. It was only accessible if you knew how.

She drove up the rough track and into her garage - just a wooden shed to the curious. Taking her bags through the adjoining door to the cabin kitchen she left them before racing back to the car. She unscrewed both license plates and replaced them with one of many plates she kept – just in case. She hid them behind a loose log in the wall and replaced the sacking which hid it. Sable closed the huge shed doors from the outside, placing some matured logs against them before hefting a couple of half full water butts in front of them so the shed looked unused. She stood for a few moments listening to the sounds of the wild animals in the forest.

Satisfied no-one had followed her she kicked the sand to hide her foot and tyre marks before going round to the front door of the cabin to let herself in. Placing a huge iron bar across the inside of the door, bolting and double locking it, she waited in silence for a moment. She'd already checked every window from the outside, ensuring the iron shutters were good and the locks on the inside were strong. She did the same with the only other exit door. All was good. The trap door in the kitchen was well concealed and should she need to make a quick escape the hinges were well maintained and oil lamps were dotted throughout the tunnel underneath to light her way, enabling a smooth get-away to an opening deep in the woods some three hundred yards away. The tunnel provided supplies and everything she might need should she be forced to abandon her cabin. She'd found the tunnel by chance when replacing the original flooring. It was if it had been built just for her. No-one knew she owned the cabin. No-one ever would.

She was tired, the sun was coming up and she needed a few hours' sleep before heading into Big Bear Lake to the diner and grocery store where she could get a decent meal and some supplies.

Chapter Five

There was a film crew in the parking lot of the grocery store when she arrived for her supplies. Tables were set out all over the lot and grass verges and the crew appeared to be taking a meal break, their voices rattling round inside Sweet Sable's head, even though she tried to blot them out, busy planning how she was going to get back at Jack.

'What gives with all the action in the parking lot?' Sweet Sable asked the deeply tanned proprietor as he handed her groceries to her.

'Hollywood's come calling again,' he told the blonde in the dark glasses. 'Making a movie called *'Gone with the Wind.'* He sniffed, 'not enough we got all 'em movie stars buying up real estate on the mountain, they gotta bring their work back with them.'

'Yeah, they seem to like it up here,' Sweet Sable said, as she allowed the old man to open the door for her. 'I guess it's good for business.'

'You bet,' he said, closing the door. So, the blonde was back. Good job he didn't have to rely on her for business, he'd go broke in no time. The old man could count on the fingers of one hand the number of times he'd ever seen her.

Sweet Sable's gaze swept across the parking lot and over the crew. No-one seemed overly interested in her so she got in her car to head home. She did a double take leaving the parking lot. Vivien Leigh and Clarke Gable were crossing in front of her. *'Gone with the Wind'* must be some big budget movie with them in it, she mused. With lots of movie folk milling around the place another stranger shouldn't attract any attention, she thought, so she should be able to move around without standing out too much. Anyway, she could pass for a stranger because she was never herself when dropping in to town, she mused, as she drove home. Few had ever seen her as a blonde, a redhead, or any other hair colour frequently enough to recognise her. She was a chameleon.

*****

Back at her cabin, groceries sorted and with a cup of coffee on the table next to her, she sorted through the documents she'd stolen from Jack's safe. He was dirty. He was on the take from the studios, promising he'd release land to them for building their lots. And he promised real estate developers land availability once he'd been elected. They were paying for his political campaign in return for his vote on issues they had interests in. He'd been taking back-handers for years from mobsters in Vegas too. Jack had kept records of all his transactions obviously not trusting an accountant or bank to keep his books safe. Jack clearly hadn't reckoned on someone like Sweet Sable in his life.

Sable giggled to herself. Jack was clueless about her or any of her 'skills.' Lucky for her she'd overheard a conversation he'd had with one of the trusted flunkies always hanging around him, alerting her to something fishy going on, and she knew she'd struck lucky; her instincts about Jack were right. She'd found a way to make some big bucks; even a little revenge was going to be doubly sweet.

Chapter Six

'What do you mean, she's skipped?' Jack yelled at the thug in front of him who was sweating like a Chinaman in a restaurant kitchen. 'How?'

'I dunno she just skipped.' The man didn't meet Jack's eyes, hanging his head, terrified. 'She got wind, is all.'

'Got wind? How did that happen?' Jack walked around his solid oak desk and stood almost toe to toe with his flunky.

'I belled her, told her nicely she gotta give your stuff back like you said. But she hung up. I went round there to persuade her but she was gone already. Took off when I wasn't watching.'

Jack sat down again and glared at the man in front of him who shifted uneasily. 'I said scare the crap out of her *If* she didn't play ball right away.' He thumped the desk. 'I meant get her to understand the implications straight off if she didn't give. I didn't say send her running. I didn't tell you to take your eyes off her, not even to hit the john.'

'She won't be far, where she gonna go? We'll soon find her boss.' The man waited. It could go either way now, he knew. His life was in the balance. He could end up with a ruby necklace like Luigi who'd messed up big time last year. He was lucky he didn't have to do the hit, he'd been friends with Luigi since they ran numbers for the mob back in Vegas years ago. Who'd make his hit, he wondered, shivering in-spite of his sweat. He didn't know how much more he could take. Numbers were one thing, but killing: he'd had a belly full.

'Your last chance, hear me? Your one and only chance. You find her, you get my stuff back and then you get rid of her. No mess, no noise, no-one will ever know what happened - and I mean no-one - not even me. Got it?' Jack leaned over the desk and shoved his face right into the sweating man's face. 'Got it?' he shouted again.

'Sure boss, don't worry, she's history already, no sweat. We'll get it all back.'

'There's no *We* about it. You do this on your own, you tell no-one and don't tell me about it either. Do it, do it quietly and keep your mouth shut or you will be meeting Luigi faster than you can blink. You leave my stuff in my mailbox and I'll make sure you get paid. Then you disappear. Now get out of my sight.'

Carlo ran from the room before his boss changed his mind. Now he had to find the broad before she did damage with what she took. His head ached with fear and worry. He'd be watching his own back from now on. He didn't trust his boss any more than the would-be politician trusted him.

Chapter Seven

Sable started to make plans. She read and re-read the documents she'd stolen from Jack's safe trying to work out how best to use them for the maximum reward. Sending them to the Governor was too risky. He and Jack knew each other and she wasn't sure if he'd pay up to save Jack's career aspirations. He might even try to snuff her out. She considered blackmailing Jack. A nice long-term earner, it was tempting. Well, he'd got a hit out on her anyway, that much was obvious following the phone call so she didn't see what difference having another bullseye on her back made. Her plans for the future needed money, lots of it. Just one more job should do it. She poured herself three fingers of bourbon and returned to the couch tucking her legs underneath her. She sipped, contemplating her options. Sable knew she had to cover herself more than she'd ever needed to before. She knew it was only a matter of time before any one of her marks found her. Over the years she'd mostly worked alone, rarely involving anyone else. Well, there was someone she used if necessary but even he was dispensable if push came to shove. Even he didn't know her true identity.

She couldn't remain hidden forever. She wouldn't spend her life hiding, watching her back. This was the last job and it had to pay big-time. Jack had to suffer and pay – and boy, was he going to pay!

Chapter Eight

Jack Brady was a creature of habit and Sable knew his habits inside out – she'd been one. Every Tuesday afternoon he'd visit the Sand and Pool Club at the Beverly Hills hotel. He loved to socialise with movie stars such as Fred Astaire and Cesar Romero, mostly because they always had a beautiful woman somewhere nearby. Sable had his number. He was always on the pick-up there just as he was at nightclub stage doors. The guy was a serial cheat.

After he'd chewed the fat with the social elite of Hollywood he'd hit the private bars where there was always a game going on. He was utterly convinced he couldn't lose, that he was a big winner – which wasn't that often - but it didn't seem to put him off. And he'd bet on anything; even two lizards crawling up a wall. Jack was also a sore loser and he'd throw a tantrum if he lost. His flunkies often had to come and prise him away before his antics got into the Press and his political career got shot down before it got started.

In the early hours he'd drive to the apartment he kept just off Sunset Boulevard which Sable knew his wife didn't have a clue he had. His minders were usually given the night off but Jack was rarely alone. Sable often spent time with him there and lately she'd watched him take the office candy there. She'd spied on him once she got wind she had competition.

Hair covered with another wig - this time dark black and short in the style of Louise Brooks, the actress she'd seen with John Wayne in the movie, 'Overland Stage Raiders,' last year - Sable looked at herself in the mirror. She'd changed the shape of her eyebrows and the line of her lips using stage make-up she'd acquired over the years. The night before she'd taken a stroll near the movie crew trailers. She'd noticed that the make-up and costume trailers were rarely closed at night, especially if they were filming night scenes. There was a watchman who was supposed to keep his eyes open on the lot but he was drunk by about 9 pm like many of the crew, and some of the cast, who weren't needed until morning.

There was little to do once it got dark on the mountain and around the lake, and with a 4 am call for cast breakfast most were only too glad to hit the hay early, which was fine by Sable, it suited her.

She'd waited until the night crew were otherwise engaged and entered the appropriate trailers helping herself to make-up and a couple of wigs. She'd easily left without anyone knowing. Whether or not the losses would be noticed she didn't know or care. It was an opportunity too good to miss and she'd added her spoils to her growing assortment of disguises, wigs, make-up, and costumes. She had an outfit for every occasion and *'person'* she'd become when necessary.

Sable even took some body padding which would increase her dress size considerably and might come in handy one day, but not now. Now she had to look drop-dead gorgeous. She studied herself in the mirror again.

She was ready.

Chapter Nine

Tuesday afternoon like clockwork Jack settled himself beside the poolside bar at the Sand and Pool Club and sipped his Bees Knees cocktail. Something Sable had got him hooked on when he was with her – not to mention the sex. He'd been hooked on that until he employed Lola; Lola was younger and she knew no bounds. He chuckled thinking about Lola and her taste for South Side Fizz. It was a favourite of Al Capone's apparently, though how she knew that he couldn't imagine. She didn't have a head for it and that suited him. She could drink the South Side dry as far as he was concerned, it made her pliable.

Lola was meeting him at the apartment later that evening. His mouth watered at the thought. Meantime his attention was taken with a leggy dame who had taken one of the poolside loungers.

She had short black hair cut kind of cute and everything was in the right place: from her painted toe-nails to the gold necklace which rested on her creamy white bosom, catching his eye every time she moved. And boy could the dame move. She passed him a few times as she wandered around the pool in her swimsuit trailing her towel which, as far as he could see, never got wet. She was a looker. An eyeful. He started to toy with the idea of talking to her but she never once glanced at him. The dame seemed very smitten with one of the waiters who hadn't taken his eyes off her since she sashayed in.

At last the dame sat down again casually glancing his way. He nodded, she smiled, and turned her attention to a book, sipping her drink now and again as she read. She crossed her long legs a few times and once he caught her looking at him over the top of her sunglasses. He grinned to himself. She'd noticed him. He waved the waiter over, 'what's she drinking?' he asked, pointing to the girl.

'She's been drinking Mary Pickford's so far sir,' he answered looking at the girl a little longer than necessary.

'Get her one, on me,' Jack said, shoving a couple of bills at the waiter. 'Tell her she's welcome to join me if she wants. It's not good drinking alone.'

The drink and message delivered, the dark-haired girl nodded, smiled, and rose from her lounger carrying her glass over to where he'd risen to his feet. She kept her dark glasses on to shield the glare from the overhead sun.

She smiled a secret smile at her success.

Jack patted himself on the back mentally. Lola would get the flick just for tonight and no mistake. He'd call her later.

*****

'You don't look like you're from LA, where're you from?' Jack asked her as she sat beside him, enjoying her lingering handshake and her smile loaded with promise.

'Sweden,' she said, with a heavy accent. 'I am Freda.' Sable had always been good at accents and was particularly fond of Sweden which she'd read up on following a little sting she'd perpetrated upon an unsuspecting rich Brazilian actor many years before.

'Where do you come from?' she asked him wiggling into a more comfortable position on the lounger next to him.

'California born and bred.' Jack cleared his throat and took a deep slug of his cocktail. Swedish. He'd heard they were feisty. The women were encouraged to express themselves and be independent, just like Ingrid Bergman. A woman out to have some fun he was sure.

Freda and Jack chatted for about an hour, flirting outrageously with each other. The waiter hovered and supplied more drinks, a sullen expression on his handsome face. Jack left to make a phone call for a few minutes and Freda grinned to herself. Everything was going to plan. Jack had taken the bait.

'You're enjoying this too much,' the waiter whispered, handing Freda another cocktail. Unknown to Jack his companion's drinks had been watered down. Jack's had more alcohol than the recipe demanded. 'It's taking too long.'

'Jealousy is never attractive,' she replied watching the entrance. 'Just serve and wait. He's on the hook. I've just got to get him to want to leave when I want to – no sweat.' Freda sipped her drink and eyed the muscular man appreciatively. He'd always been fun and useful whenever she needed a companion for a sting. However, recently she was in two minds whether to keep him or get rid of him after this sting.

'I'll go to the little girl's room - that's your signal to get to the apartment and you'll have half an hour max. The key works, I've tested it – he hasn't changed the locks. Let yourself in and get everything set up. I'll keep him busy. You know where to hide.'

'Well hurry up. I can't stand this much longer.' He took the key.

Jack returned having brushed Lola off, telling her, 'something's come up and I can't see you tonight.'

Lola was disappointed but she knew business came first. She tried not to sound disappointed but she wondered what was so important it hadn't come through the office, through her.

16

'All right Jack, next Tuesday I guess.' She couldn't keep the edge out of her voice. All this skulking around was driving her nuts. She wanted more. Jack was going to have to take her seriously, take their relationship seriously, and soon. Or his wife was going to get a nasty shock.

Chapter Ten

The movie extra turned waiter turned whatever he needed to be - whenever The Red Siren asked him - let himself into Jack's apartment and moved quickly across the large room to where he'd been told the master bedroom would be. He looked around, found the walk-in closet with the slatted front Sable had told him about and went about setting up his Bolex equipment, borrowed from a gumshoe he knew, no questions asked. He tested it a few times and happy that the angles were right, made himself as comfortable as possible and then settled down to wait.

About ten minutes later he heard the front door open and voices. He held his breath. His knees screaming for relief he shifted to relieve the pain before the couple came into the bedroom. He checked his equipment and strained his ears, expectant and nervous.

'I'll make some drinks and bring them in,' an obviously drunk Jack shouted. 'You make yourself right at home in there, I won't be long.'

'You OK?' she whispered close to the closet door. 'Everything ready?'

'Yeah, just get on with it. To get the right angle I'm kneeling on the floor and my knees are killing me.'

'Too much football wrecks your joints they say.'

'Cut the jawing and get on with it,' he hissed back. Very unhappy about what was going to happen if everything went to plan. 'Make with some music, this thing is noisy.'

'He'll be too busy to hear anything,' she laughed as she began to undress. Dirk grunted.

'Stop drooling and concentrate,' she added, feeling her co-conspirator's eyes upon her. 'You've seen it all before Dirk.'

Dirk had indeed. That didn't make it any easier for him. She knew he was in love with her and how hard it was going to be. They'd played some dodgy games before, stiffed a few marks and it never got to him, but never before had he been asked to actually film her with another guy. She really was pushing it. The guy was really asking for it.

*****

'Let's keep the light on, it makes it more interesting,' Freda said when Jack had undressed and made his way to the bed. She wanted Dirk to get everything as clearly as possible so there couldn't be any dispute.

18

Jack was in no mood to argue. She handed him another drink and sipped hers slowly watching him beneath her lashes.

The would-be politician was unconscious long before he got to fully devour the delights of his Swedish conquest but the movie Dirk was able to record had enough to blow the guy's career right out of the water.

Dirk packed his camera away and glowered at the snoring man, 'I could kill him.'

'Grow up.' Sable dressed, removed her glass from beside the bed and any traces of herself in the apartment. 'Dirk, wipe the closet down and the apartment door, just in case you've left any dabs.'

Dirk set about his chore and when he was satisfied he let himself out of the apartment after confirming he'd meet Sable in a couple of days when he'd copied the movie. Unaware that he was being watched and followed he got into his car and drove to his apartment on La Brea.

After Dirk left Sable set about rifling the apartment. She took papers, jewellery, money, even some gold, and anything else she could carry. She cleaned Jack out – well, almost cleaned him out. The best was yet to come.

Jack's henchman, Carlo, had been watching the apartment because he knew that Jack would be there on a Tuesday night at some point. He was going to waste his boss. He couldn't take the strain of worrying about being hit himself. Carlo couldn't find the broad and he was terrified. He needed just one chance when Jack was alone. But he'd not only seen a new broad go in with Jack, he'd seen some guy go inside earlier. He continued watching anyway and sure enough an hour later the guy came out carrying something he'd taken in with him earlier. He decided to follow him.

*****

Sable left a note with disguised handwriting for the unconscious Jack. *'Didn't want to wake you, thanks for a fun time. See you around,'* and she left. She knew where to find him but he hadn't managed to find out anything more about her other than her name. He wouldn't even remember his performance for the camera which Sable had choreographed so that his face was in the frame even when his body wasn't. He was instantly recognisable. She was just a female form. Luckily she didn't have any scars or other identifying marks so she was certain she couldn't be identified and Dirk never filmed her face.

Happy with what she'd achieved Sable left the apartment making sure she wasn't observed. She couldn't wait until Dirk had the movie ready, when the fun would really begin.

Chapter Eleven

Carlo watched as Dirk entered the La Brea apartment building. It was respectable and well maintained and Carlo tried to recall anything he might know about the place, but he couldn't. He hung around for half an hour, then went inside. The desk clerk was asleep, his head resting on his arms at his desk. Carlo couldn't see any keys with names attached and didn't want to attract attention to himself by waking the clerk and asking, so he decided to call it quits and go back to Jack's apartment. Was this guy a hitman? Should he be watching him too?

The broad could be leaving any time soon if Jack followed his usual routine of kicking them out before dawn - he'd better hurry back to Jack's.

Carlo got as comfortable as he could in his car parked opposite his boss's apartment and prepared for a long wait.

The broad hadn't reappeared by dawn and Carlo was getting cramp. Perhaps he'd missed her. Curiosity got the better of him and he decided to go up to the apartment before too many people were about. Carlo knew where his boss kept his spare key – they all knew – in case of emergencies. He felt around the base of the aspidistra outside the door and removed the key. He'd have to deal with the broad as well, he thought, if she was still there.

Carlo moved stealthily towards the master bedroom surprised to find the door open and Jack lying in bed snoring soundly. There wasn't any sign of a broad in the whole apartment. She must've left when he was following the guy. He found Sable's note, smiling wryly as he read it. She hadn't had the time of her life by the looks of it. He put the note in his pocket.

Moving beside the bed he looked at Jack uncertain what to do next, his resolve wobbling. He looked around, took a deep breath – nothing would change - he had to do it. He wanted his life back. Carlo made up his mind. He was going to New York on the Greyhound - he had family there running the docks.

The apartment was empty, no-one had seen him enter and if he hurried, no-one would see him leave. He always wore gloves so when he placed the gun in Jack's hand and placed it against the unconscious man's head, pressing his finger to the trigger, he knew that the natural conclusion would be that Jack had killed himself – at least that is what he hoped. He winced at the sound of the shot and looked at what was left of Jack's brains scattered across the pillows.

Chapter Twelve

It was all over the evening editions, headlines news with graphic photos of the scene of the apparent suicide of would-be politician Jack Grady, pillar of the establishment and known benefactor to charities and good causes. Speculation was rife as to why he'd kill himself but according to the cops it was an open and shut case. No-one else was involved.

The Establishment and his business colleagues came out in force to sing his praises and give their condolences to his grieving widow and family.

Lola gave tear-jerking accounts of what a great boss he was to work for, how everyone loved him. She was already thinking about telling her story to some of the scandal rags – they'd pay she was sure and maybe she'd get some movie interest. Every cloud, she thought, sobbing as another camera flashed.

Sable and Dirk sat in his La Brea apartment unsure what to do next. Both accused the other of killing their mark. 'You said you wanted to kill him,' she'd yelled at him. 'He wasn't capable of doing it himself, he was out for the count for several more hours at least.'

'Yeah, well you were with him after I left, how do I know you didn't bump him off?'

'Don't be dumb, I needed him alive you lame brain.'

'Well if he was too out of it how did he kill himself? You tell me.' Dirk glared across the room at her.

'I dunno, someone must've done it, got in after we left and off'd him.' Sable was furious her last sting had gone south. 'Shut up, let me think.'

If someone had gone into the apartment Sable needed to know who. Had they seen her and Dirk, or had they arrived later? She had no idea how to find out and she didn't want to draw attention by asking questions.

'We'll wait and see what happens, keep low for a while, see if anyone crawls out of the woodwork.' She decided.

'I'll see you tomorrow afternoon, disappear until then. We'll see how the movie turns out and make plans.' Sable drove back to Big Bear. She needed peace and quiet. Dirk didn't argue, he was thinking too.

Chapter Thirteen

'What do you wanna do about the movie?' Dirk asked after they'd watched the film of Sable with Jack. They were at the Vista movie theatre owned by a friend of Dirk's, who'd let them use it in private. It was well known for soft-porn movies so no-one turned a hair when the blonde dame with the hunky guy turned up, movie in hand. It took all sorts.

Dirk could hardly watch Sable with Jack again. He felt sick.

'His wife's our target. Those development companies he dealt with – I don't trust them not to play hard-ball – they're too powerful. Same with the movie studios.'

'Right, you got my drift too. Steer clear.' Dirk felt relief. He knew what they had on Jack was dynamite but with all that knowledge came some serious heat. They'd be dead meat in no time but the wife, she was loaded and she'd want to keep Jack's dirty secrets from getting out. She was old money, society, and scandal would ruin her and her family. 'She'll pay.'

Sable wasn't going to give up, Jack owed her. Whoever killed him might come after her and Dirk if they'd been following them. It crossed her mind it might even be a rival of Jack's, getting the dirt on him. But it worried her she didn't know, hadn't seen it coming.

'Yeah, she's loaded, got her own money and she has her kids to protect.' Sable had decided to keep Dirk around after-all following a lot of thought. She'd told him earlier that he could have half shares from Jack and if he wanted to hang around after, that was good with her.

'Of course I do, I told you long ago, I love you, baby. We're made for each other.'

'I'm tired of finding marks, setting the stings up, having to keep moving on - becoming someone new.'

Dirk nodded, 'yeah, me too, baby.'

'I might carry on singing, I enjoy it. I didn't realise it until recently.'

'You're a great singer Sable, the punters love you.'

'I've seen an ad for nightclub singers in Acapulco, it would be a start.' Dirk would be handy for muscle. She'd play it straight this time. Have a life. If she got bored, she'd move on.

'You could come. They make movies there if you wanted work and there're great beaches too.' Sable knew she'd miss the excitement of her 'other' life - there was nothing like it - but she knew she couldn't keep it up much longer.

'Sure I will, no question, but first, we need to deal with the wife.' Bringing them both back to the present. 'Let's tell her all about her sainted Jack.'

Chapter Fourteen

Jack's widow Jennifer wasn't stupid, she knew the score. His death had shaken her, grieved her children, but she just felt relief. She knew about his affairs, turning a blind eye for the sake of her family and reputation. Divorce in her family was not an option, the shame was not tolerable. If Jack hadn't died when he did she'd have arranged a little accident for him herself, eventually. His flunkies knew which side their bread was buttered. Money spoke volumes and she was prepared to pay. Her patience had been running thin. Now she played her part in public but in private she wanted to dance.

The urge to dance soon disappeared. The package in the mail with footage of Jack with some floozy pulled her up short, so did the request for an enormous one-off payment to ensure silence. At first she considered calling the cops, her lawyer, or one of Jack's thugs, but photo after photo of documents showing crooked deals with studio heads, real estate companies, even people she'd never heard of made her stop and think. Her family would never recover from the scandal and shame that Jack's exposure would rain down upon them. Jennifer could afford the sums requested. She'd need originals and proof of destruction of any further copies. She reasoned that she'd probably never be sure and that blackmailers never let go, but for now she was prepared to pay. To make it go away until she and her family could move on from Jack's death. If the blackmailer came back for more, well she'd rethink things. If the blackmailer had also bumped Jack off somehow they deserved a reward. Let their demand be their payoff from a grateful widow, she decided.

Jack's widow contacted the go-between and made it clear that should she be asked for more, she'd send a hit squad. A small fortune in cash was exchanged for a movie and documents three days later. The widow held a lavish funeral with all the social elite from Hollywood, politics, and high society in attendance. Jack was dead and buried. She wanted him to stay that way.

Chapter Fifteen

The spotlight found its mark as the music started. The singer stroked the mic-stand seductively and began to sing. Forty minutes later to rapturous applause The Red Siren blew kisses to her audience and left the stage, waving off the adoring glances and offers from the Argentinian *stage door Johnnies,* as she made her way to her dressing-room.

Dirk mixed her a generous cocktail as she slipped out of her slinky gown. She flopped on the couch beside him. 'Salud y amor y tiempo para disfrutarlo.' She raised her glass to Dirk.

'Health and love and time to enjoy it, to you too,' he replied. They clinked glasses.

'Where do you want to head next? she asked, sighing deeply.

'I don't mind, anywhere is good.'

'Brazil, we said we'd go to Brazil after Acapulco, but we ended up in Cuba, which I adore, I really do, but I want to experience Brazil, the music and those rhythms.' She shivered. 'I want to sing there, to experience the atmosphere.'

'Brazil it is, I'll make the arrangements.' Dirk was happier than he'd ever been and so was Sable.

'We should raise a toast to Jack, his wife, his money, and all those lovely things I found in his apartment which have given us this new life Dirk. All those Bearer Bonds, the cash, the gold and the jewels.' She sighed deeply. 'And to all those other generous men over the years who've paid for our new life.'

Dirk and Sable stood and raised their glasses to Jack and all their other benefactors. He turned to Sable, asking, 'what is your real name? I've never known and after all this time surely you can tell me?'

She kissed him and smiled, 'you only need to know what I want you to know Dirk, it's safer for us both.'

'Everyone calls you The Red Siren or Sweet Sable, surely there's another, more intimate name I can call you now we are together permanently?' Dirk insisted.

Sable studied him for a long time and smiled slowly. 'I can only repeat it is safer you don't know. Don't ask again, let's enjoy the time we have.'

Raising her glass she repeated, 'Salud y amor y tiempo para disfrutarlo.'

Dirk raised his glass, but a shiver crept down his spine. 'Health and love and the time to enjoy it,' he repeated.

APARTMENT 206c

Chapter One

China held her breath waiting for the next crash and thud which would, as surely as night followed day, resound from the apartment next door. For three hours the yelling and shouting had gone on and she kicked herself once more for never having learned a foreign language. She would've loved to have known what the other two were shouting. The daughter she could understand; she screamed abuse at her parents in English.

She'd considered taking a course in Spanish a few years back when she was trying to 'improve' herself but chickened out when push came to shove. The new series of NCIS clashed with the class schedules and anyway it would have been winter and China didn't fancy going out on cold nights.

From what the daughter was yelling it seemed that the parents were trying to prevent her from having a relationship with a Russian boy, whom they accused of being in a gang. For once China could imagine what the parents were saying. Not that she was a parent and had to put up with wayward daughters, but she had been a daughter and had fallen out with her own parents numerous times over her latest love. Nine times out of ten her parents had been spot on and the boy she was mad about turned out to be a waste of space. Not that she ever admitted it to them. However, something made China think there was more to the rows than just an unsuitable boyfriend.

The family next door had moved in about six years ago and at first had been quiet and friendly and kept themselves to themselves. But of late all that had changed. Almost daily there were rows: screaming, shouting, crashing, and the tinkle of glass filled the once quiet corridors of the apartment block where middle-class tenants went about their business without intrusion upon their fellow occupants.

China was on nodding acquaintance with them and apart from the odd, 'Hi, how are you?' when passing in the lobby or sharing the elevator, she knew next to nothing about them, this being their only contact with each other. She ascertained that the parents were Spanish and that their daughter spoke fluent English. China assumed they were first-generation immigrants and the daughter was integrating better than they. She certainly gave the impression of the 'All American' girl from the way she spoke to her parents without any trace of an accent, her attitude and the way she dressed like her peers.

The ferocity of this recent argument convinced China that something else was going on with the family and the daughter in particular. She couldn't put her finger on it but the intensity of emotions and the violent reaction of the person who seemed to be intent upon destroying every piece of glass, crockery, and furniture in the adjoining apartment caused China to feel really fearful. Of what she had no idea. But it was fear she felt when she listened to the escalation in passions coming through the walls into her own piece of heaven.

The shouting that followed the latest session had sent a chill down her spine as she tried to concentrate on writing her novel. She found herself holding her breath, waiting. Waiting for what she hadn't a clue, but it seemed to her that a line had been crossed next door. She walked to the shared apartment wall and leaned against it trying to hear what was going on inside now that it appeared to have gone silent. Her ear began to hurt as she pressed it against her sitting room wall and she turned her head and leaned her other ear against the cool wall; nothing. Just silence.

She ran to the kitchen, grabbed a glass and used this against the wall to see if she could hear better, but all she could hear was the rapid thudding of her own heart. Putting the glass down on her coffee table she ran to her front door and looked through the spy-hole in-case there was any movement in the hall. Surely someone else had heard the racket. The area the spy-hole covered was useless, she couldn't see far enough to the right near her neighbour's door. Taking a deep breath she slowly and silently opened her door and stepped out into the hall, cautiously slipping along the wall until she came to their front door.

Chapter Two

At first all seemed silent and she wondered if they had gone out without her realising. But as she pressed her ear to their door she thought she heard muffled voices on the other side. She stepped back quickly, moving back along the wall out of sight. She waited. She dare not breathe, yet she wanted to giggle as well. She wondered how on earth she would explain herself if someone else came along and found her trying to melt into the deep red and gold flock wallpaper.

Sure enough, someone was coming. The elevator just down the hall rattled up from the ground floor and she heard the bell as it stopped and the doors opened. Feeling a bit stupid standing up against the wall dressed only in her pyjamas – her favourite writing outfit – she frantically ran for her own front door and just managed to slip inside as the recent occupant of the elevator passed by. Curious as to their identity China looked through the spy-hole and just managed to catch a glimpse of a tall dark-haired young man standing outside her neighbour's apartment. He glanced around furtively - so it seemed to China - before tapping gently on the door of the last apartment on her floor; Apartment 206c.

China eased herself out of her doorway and crept along the wall until she could see the door which was closed again. She tiptoed up to it and put her ear against it. She heard two loud pops, like champagne corks being released from their bottles. Just as she was thinking what a nosey person she must be spying on her neighbours and thinking all sorts of nonsense about them she heard a groan; an agonised groan, breathy and rattling. It reminded her of the death rattle you heard on TV shows when someone expired after being shot. There was always a gasp and the sound of the last breath leaving the body. Well, that is what she thought as she listened, fear tingling through her body, her novelist's mind alive with all sorts of nonsensical ideas as to what might be going on in the rooms behind the closed door.

Was that a sob she heard? A woman's cry followed by shuffling noises? What was going on? China felt a sense of foreboding and wondered what she should do, if anything.

A man's voice, muffled and deep, filtered through as she strained to hear what was being said. It sounded like accented English but China didn't recognise it – it must be the young man's voice, she thought. Next she heard the daughter's voice, hushed and urgent at first, and then louder and shrill - a row perhaps? More muffled words, another cry followed by what sounded like a slap and a groan. Ominously she couldn't hear either of the parents speaking. Were they still at home?

Every nerve in her body was racing, her skin felt as if it were crawling with ants as she began to fear for the family inside. She wondered if she should call the police but dismissed the idea because she hadn't proof of anything amiss. No-one else had come out of their apartments to inquire about the racket that had gone on for such a long time, stopping so suddenly, following ear-splitting screams earlier. She would only make a complete fool of herself with the police and she could just imagine how her neighbours would think of her when they discovered they were being spied upon and speculated about by their writer neighbour. Everyone would put it down to her over-active imagination and without any proof of something untoward going on she wondered how would she get the police to come out, let alone investigate.

China decided that she would have to act alone to discover what was going on in the apartment. She would inform the authorities if or when she found anything. Leaning closer to the door China tried hard to catch what was being said inside but all she could hear was a series of muffled words, thuds and scratches. She considered knocking on the door on the pretext of borrowing something but put the thought quickly aside when it occurred to her that she had never asked them for anything before, and it might arouse their suspicions and attract attention to her if she asked out of the blue like that.

She was so deep in thought she didn't realise that her foot had hit against the bottom of the door as she pressed against the wood. The noise was subtle and she hadn't heard it, but it had been heard. An eye watched her through the spy-hole.

Suddenly the door was yanked open and a tattooed arm reached out and strong thin fingers grabbed her wrist and hauled her into the apartment. China went flying on to the floor, face down, landing beside what looked like blood stains and two bulky forms hidden by blankets, lying just inside the door. Now she knew what had been going on in apartment 206c.

Chapter Three

China looked up at the man and girl standing over her, their faces filled with menace.

'Who are you?' The man grabbed her arm and pulled her to her feet roughly.

'She lives next door,' the girl said, before China could gather her thoughts. 'She's some sort of writer or whatever.'

'What does she want?' he asked, twisting China's arm behind her back and forcing her into the kitchen. 'She's a friend of yours?' he hissed at the girl. China cried out in pain as he yanked her arm further up her back.

'No, no, we're not friends, we pass in the hall is all.' The girl looked frightened. She avoided China's eyes. 'Ask her.' The girl's eyes were red and she looked as if she'd been crying. There was a large red welt across her right cheek.

The tattooed young man studied the girl for a moment as if trying to decide whether or not to believe her. He looked at China. 'She telling the truth? You don't know her, right?'

China's breath caught in her throat which had gone dry with fear, she could only nod. Her mind was racing along with her heart-rate. What the hell had she stumbled in to? She wasn't sure whether to speak or to keep quiet. She needed to work out what was going on. China held her tongue.

'What were you doing, outside?' He yanked her arm again, she cried out and he hit her across the face. 'Shut up bitch, you want the whole building in here? Now, tell me and fast, what were you doing outside the door?'

Tears streamed down China's face and blood trickled into her mouth from her cut lip. She licked her lip. 'I need - I mean - I wanted to ask if I could borrow some coffee,' she stammered. Seeing the look of disbelief cross his face, she hurriedly added, 'I haven't been to the store for a few days because I'm writing.' She didn't have any coffee so if he went into her apartment to check, he'd know she was being truthful. 'I lose track of time.'

'She does that, borrows stuff,' the girl spoke quickly. 'Mom told me she's a right pain, always forgetting to buy stuff.' She glared pointedly at China who couldn't believe her ears. Not that she was going to argue. Not that the girl's mom was going to argue; she wasn't going to argue with anyone ever again, nor was her dad. China shuddered refusing to look at what was on the hall floor.

'She's never called round when I've been here,' he said.

China nodded enthusiastically. 'Yes, she was kind to me,' she whispered looking at the floor, unable to face the man. She hoped he assumed she spoke Spanish with the parents.

'You should've gone to the store. Big mistake.' The young man shoved her on to a kitchen chair. 'Now you've given me a big problem. What to do with you?'

'We could let her go, she won't tell, will you?' the girl nodded at China, 'right?'

'No, no, I won't say anything, I promise.' China brightened, she'd keep quiet if only they'd let her go. 'My lips are sealed.'

'Say anything about what?' he growled.

'Nothing, about nothing. I mean I don't know...'

'Don't take me for a fool. You're not a fool either.' He jabbed her in the chest.

China's heart sank. 'But I'll keep quiet, I promise.'

'You on your own in there?' He pointed in the direction of her apartment.

'Yes, yes I live alone.' She regretted it the moment the words left her lips. Stupid girl. 'I have friends and family visit all the time,' she added. 'I don't go out much so they visit me, all the time.' She couldn't risk endangering Louise, her room-mate, who was safely at work for now. And she didn't want him thinking she wouldn't be missed either.

'She telling the truth?' The young man stared hard at the girl.

'I don't know anything about her, Jan, I've only ever seen her in the lobby. I've never seen her with anyone, Mom never said anything about her – just she borrows stuff.'

The young man regarded her for a few moments. 'Get some rope and something to shove in her mouth,' he told the girl. 'Rope's in my backpack.' He pointed to a blue backpack sitting on the kitchen counter. 'There's gaffer tape in there, bring that.'

China felt panic rise in her throat and she coughed bile against her pyjama sleeve. 'Please, I won't tell anyone, please, don't do this,' she pleaded, dread creeping into every pore. 'What are you going to do with me?'

'Shut the fuck up and let me think.' His first thought was kill her and worry about getting rid of her and the others later. He'd get the guys to sort that out but he was worried about his girlfriend. She was too emotional and unpredictable, could he risk it? The author had heard enough to come nosing around when he'd shut the parents up. Who else might be curious?

'Jan, we can let her go, she won't tell, she's frightened, honest, she won't tell.' The girl handed rope and tape to her co-killer. 'Will this do?' She held a

32

small piece of material in her hand which China dreaded having shoved in her mouth. China fought hard to control her rising terror, her eyes moving frantically around the room, fruitlessly seeking a saviour.

'Tie her up and shove that in her mouth, then tape it.' He went into the main room, his cell phone in hand.

The girl carried out her instructions and as she bent over China she whispered, 'I won't tie it too tight. If you get a chance, get out, get away.' She grimaced and added, 'I'm sorry.'

China ached with questions and tried to speak but she couldn't. The young man watched them both as he spoke on the phone. He spoke in a foreign language, rapidly and loudly, all the time his eyes on the women. The girl seemed as clueless as China as to what he was saying although she was obviously straining hard, trying to latch on to a word which she might understand, just as China was. Seeing the expression in China's eyes the girl whispered, 'Russian, he's speaking Russian.'

Great, China thought, a Russian Spy ring is all I need. Her imagination went into over-drive briefly as she imagined Matt Damon or Daniel Craig crashing through the front door to rescue her. The man's voice shook her out of her revelry.

'I've gotta go out, you keep an eye on her; don't let her move, don't talk to her, understand me, or you'll join her, got it?' He put a jacket on and moved to the hall door, pointing to what China was now certain were the girl's parents. 'Don't touch them either, understood? They'll be moved after dark.' He glanced at China, 'with her,' he added menacingly.

'I've got it, I won't. How long will you be gone?' The girl avoided looking at the blankets on the floor, bloodied, covering the dead. She tried not to shake. Hold it together, don't lose it now, she told herself.

'As long as it takes, I've got some stuff to take care of.' He stood over the girl who was much shorter than he and kissed her forehead. 'Be a good girl because if you're not you know who'll come for you don't you?'

'I'm not stupid Jan, you don't need to keep telling me.'

'Right, make sure you do otherwise I won't be able to protect you. And keep her quiet; any trouble, use the knife.'

'What? I can't, I've never – you can't expect me to...'

'Then you better keep her quiet, for both your sakes.' He opened the apartment door cautiously and after checking the hall was clear, he glanced at the women and left.

Chapter Four

China's neighbour waited a few seconds, then said, 'do you have a cell phone in your PJ pockets? If you do I need it.' She approached China and reached out to pat her down, something Jan hadn't thought to do. 'I never go anywhere without mine, even in my PJs.' She fumbled in both pockets and produced China's cell.

'Good, and full battery too, great.'

Her captive watched helpless, a dozen questions flooding her mind. Curiosity began to replace raw fear, for now. She felt that as long as Jan was gone, she had a chance. The girl was a mystery. What was going on? What sort of human being would be complicit in her own parent's murder? Perhaps she should be more terrified of the girl and what she was capable of, but somehow she wasn't; yet.

'I know what you're thinking, but you're wrong. I never thought this would happen.' The girl pointed to the covered bodies, the blood splattered hall wall. She gulped and wiped her eyes with the back of her hand. 'You don't understand.'

China tried to speak but her words were muffled by the gag. She shook head, her eyes focused on the apartment door. Take this goddamn gag off and untie me, she screamed into the gag, but the girl wasn't listening. She'd gone into the other room, making a call. China strained to hear what she was saying but the blood raging in her ears rendered it near impossible. The girl seemed to be listening to someone for the longest time and spoke only a few words after her initial dialogue. Finally, she hung up and came back into the kitchen. She took a large cook's knife from the knife block.

China shrank back in her chair convinced she was going to pass out with terror. She never took her eyes off the knife as the girl approached her slowly. She stood in front of her captive, chewing her lip. China held her breath.

The girl regarded China for a few moments as if making her mind up. 'I'm gonna tell you something and then take your gag off. You keep quiet when I do that or I will have to kill you, understood?' She leaned over China, the knife pointed at her throat. China nodded, relieved the horrid material was coming out of her bloodied mouth. With one strong rip the gaffer tape came off leaving China's lips red and sore, the gag came out next. China coughed and gasped.

'Right, now listen up.' The girl kept an eye on the apartment door. 'I need to trust you, can I?'

34

'Yes, yes you can,' China squeaked, her cut lip swollen and raw from the gag. 'Please, let me go, I won't tell.'

'Shut up and listen, this is important and I don't know how long we've got before Jan comes back.' She pointed the knife at her prisoner. 'You want to stay alive you do as I say, no question, just do it, OK?'

China nodded, glimpsing just a chink of hope in what she heard.

'Jan is Russian Mafia, know what I'm saying? He's a killer, a brutal killer. See what he did to my folks? He'd do that to us both if he had to. Don't forget that.' The girl moved behind China and began to untie her. 'I left the knots loose in-case I couldn't help you. If you'd pulled hard it would have undone.' She gathered the rope and put it on the table.

'I'm undercover FBI – know what I'm saying – working a huge, I mean huge, drug smuggling case. Jan is one of the cogs in a very big wheel and I've been cultivating him as my boyfriend to get near to the big guys.' As she spoke she opened the trash can in the corner of the kitchen and removed the full plastic bag. Pushing her hand down inside the can she extracted a gun with an ammunition box. Replacing the trash she turned to China. 'What's your name, we never got introduced?'

'China.'

'Well China, I'm Agent Serra. I guess you never knew my folks, they were the best.'

'I heard them arguing with you, I guess it was you, about your boyfriend, that's all I know of them, and we used to say hello in the lobby sometimes.' She glanced towards the hall. 'I'm sorry...'

'They didn't know anything about Jan and my case, they just hated him on sight, they didn't know I was undercover until...,' she sighed heavily. 'They had great instincts.' She was loading the gun as she spoke. 'Unfortunately for them they got too protective and Dad followed him, unknown to me, and saw him and some of his gang delivering drugs to a supplier. He had no idea what he'd wandered into. He always thought Jan was married or a no good hood, small-time stuff, but this...'

China stood on wobbly legs, deeply shocked. She cleared her throat. 'If your dad knew this why didn't he report it or tell you?'

'He didn't get chance. When he came home and told Mom they rowed, I heard them in the bedroom. At first I thought he was going to come out and lecture me, we'd have another row and he'd tell me to drop Jan. But he didn't. He started to call the cops and I had to stop him. I grabbed the phone and Mom started yelling at me and we struggled – you heard it I guess. Dad pulled her off me and started shouting about my crooked boyfriend, killer of young kids, making them addicts and well, you get the picture. They hadn't a clue what would happen – I didn't.' The FBI agent grabbed her jacket and moved to the door. 'Come with me, quietly.'

'You killed your parents?' China couldn't take it in. 'Oh my god!'

'Shut up, no I didn't, of course not. Jan killed them. He rang me during the row and heard them both kicking off at me down the phone. They speak - spoke Spanish – and very little English - Jan understands some Spanish and could tell something bad had happened. I told him they were on at me for going out with a Russian and wanted us to break up. Jan said he was coming over to talk to them, persuade them to back off about us being together. I tried to put him off but he doesn't live too far from here.' She placed her fingers over her lips and listened at the door. 'I couldn't get them to leave before he came. Stubborn as hell,' she whispered.

'Why didn't you tell your bosses what happened, they'd have stepped in surely?' China followed the Agent to the door, keeping her voice low.

'I didn't get time to let my boss know, it all happened too fast.' Biting her lip she added, 'I just had time to tell my parents I was working a case and Jan was my target - my way into the gang, to the head guy. I tried to explain we'd gone too far to quit now, the case was almost air-tight, that I just needed a little more time to nail the lot of them - that they had to forget what they knew. We rowed again, they grabbed me and we struggled. I was trying to get my gun, to be able to protect them before Jan turned up, but Mom kept grabbing me and shouting. They never wanted me to join the FBI, they worried themselves sick about it. During the row, Jan arrived.' The girl's eyes filled with tears, 'I told them to keep quiet, not mention what they knew, but Dad lost it when Jan knocked and raced to the door before I could stop him...'

China gasped and squeezed her eyes shut trying to process everything. Opening them she slowly moved past the two bodies on the floor by the door. She shuddered. Jan killed both parents, brutally, and his 'girlfriend' appeared to have no qualms about helping him to cover his crime up and help remove their bodies. You couldn't make it up.

'Why didn't you stop him?'

'I didn't get chance, I never got to my gun. Dad opened the door with Mom behind him. I don't know what they thought they'd do but as he walked in Jan shot them both, point blank, then turned the gun towards me,' her voice quivered. 'The arrogant shit believes I love him more than my folks and I let him think that. I couldn't do anything for them, so I decided to get on with the job.' She grabbed China's arm. 'Time for grief and revenge later.'

Speechless, China gawked at the girl in disbelief. Cold bitch!

'Follow me, we're getting out of here before Jan comes back. I'll tell him you needed the john and over-powered me. He thinks I'm a brainless barmaid. We met in one of the Mafia-owned clubs where his gang hang out, where I was planted to pick up intelligence on them.' She pulled the door open slowly and checked the hall was clear. 'I've spoken to my chief and if I can get you out of the building, I'll come back and wait for Jan.'

'You can't be serious! He'll kill you if he thinks you let me escape. Why've you got to come back, can't they just arrest him for your parents, for their...what happened to them?'

'The case is on-going, they want me to carry on as long as he believes in me.' The FBI agent cautiously led the way along the corridor, China tight on her heels.

'But your parents, the FBI know they're - you know...' China whispered in disbelief.

The Agent stopped and turned to China, gun in hand. 'I can't help them and what would be the point of stopping now? We need to avenge them and everyone else they've killed otherwise they've died in vain. Now shut up and follow me, we're not safe here.'

Chapter Five

Avoiding the elevator Agent Serra led China down the stairs, slowly, keeping the gun in front of her, eyes constantly scanning the stair-well as they moved between floors. Suddenly she stopped, her body stiffening. She turned to China, her finger over her lips. She signalled that China remain still. China froze. The women could hear muffled male voices somewhere beneath them. Agent Serra put China's cell - which she'd kept - to silent, and sent a text to her Chief. Who was it on the stairs?

After what seemed way too long the reply came: he didn't know, a resident perhaps. He told them to sit tight whilst they investigated. Agent Serra replied they were in the 3rd floor stairwell and would wait unless the voices moved upwards towards them. 'We wait for the all-clear,' she mouthed to China whose legs were shaking.

'What's wrong?' China mouthed back.

'Boss is checking our exit,' her companion mimed. She leaned over the stair-rail checking below and above them. Just in-case. 'Sit down,' she told China. China obeyed relieved to be off her wobbly legs.

China's cell vibrated. Glancing at it the agent whispered to China, 'all clear, just residents. Let's go.'

The journey to the ground floor was slow but thankfully uneventful. Cautiously Agent Serra pushed the fire door open and stuck her head around it, quickly scanning the lobby. The concierge was not at his desk. She closed the door and texted her boss; where was he? Her boss replied he must be in the john, keep coming; all clear. The Agent didn't reply, instead, she pushed the locking bar in place and leaned against the door, thinking. China nudged her, her expression quizzical.

'Something's not right, we're not going out this way,' she mouthed.

'Why? How do you know?'

'Gut instinct. The concierge isn't there and he should be.'

'Perhaps he's in the restroom?'

'He needs to be at his station to keep an eye out for Jan. My boss arranged it. Now isn't a good time to relieve himself.' Serra bit her lip, her mind racing. She looked at China's cell then made a call. 'Let's go back up a floor,' she whispered to China, 'quick, quietly.'

They both ran up the stairs and China waited as the young Agent whispered into the phone again, her face anxious as she listened to the reply. She ended the call.

'What?'

'A colleague, checking stuff for me. She'll text back. We stay put.' Serra leaned over the stair-rails, checking above and below stairwells. So far so good. The cell vibrated and Serra moved away from China to read the message. She texted back, waited, and read the reply before putting the cell in her pocket.

'It's not good. Whoever I thought I was texting with earlier, it wasn't my boss. He's disappeared along with two other agents who were across the road and the one downstairs in the lobby, waiting for you. Someone has been using his cell to get us outside.' She signalled for China to follow her as she moved up to the next floor. 'I think my cover's blown, we need to find another way out of here.'

China paused, taking it all in. 'You mean we can't get out of here. We're stuck?' She tried to keep her voice low but panic was rising in her throat. 'Why can't the FBI help us?'

'They're on it, believe me, but they can't just rush the building when there are other residents to consider.' Yet the young agent wasn't sure at all. She wondered if anyone other than her colleague was aware of the situation – who could be trusted?

'You think Jan has rumbled you, he's after us both?' China stopped and gripped the stair-rail. 'I feel sick.'

'Not as sick as Jan will make you believe me.' Serra grabbed China's hand and almost pulled her upstairs. 'Any other ways out of this building I don't know about?'

'No, well, not on this floor as you know, but there's a fire-escape outside my bedroom window, it's old and rusty - we're not supposed to use it.'

'Let's do it, back to your apartment – now!'

Chapter Six

They raced as quietly as possible up several flights of stairs, China trying to keep pace with the fitter Agent. Panting, she stood behind Serra as the agent cautiously opened the door to China's floor, easing her head around it, scanning the length of the hall. Thankfully the building didn't have CCTV on the residential floors and stair-wells Serra had remembered earlier. Once happy the hall was deserted, she beckoned China to follow her.

'Give me your key, stay close behind me, don't make a sound.'

China handed it over and held her breath as she almost hugged the FBI agent's back. Gently Serra inserted the key and turned it, gingerly opening the door, her gun ready. After a moment she eased herself inside and pulled China in after her. So far so good. Gently closing the door she indicated that China stay near it as she moved around the apartment, checking they were alone. Satisfied, she locked the door and fixed the various locks into place.

'Got a landline?' She moved towards the bedroom and the fire-escape.

'No, I don't, just my cell.'

'What about another cell, or computer?' She stood to one side of the bedroom window and looked down on the rusting metal eye-sore passing for a means of escape. Not good.

'Only my laptop, I use it mainly for writing.' China pointed to her bed. It lay where she'd left it a lifetime ago, it seemed.

'Internet?'

'Yes, I use it for Google and stuff.'

'Get me online, fast.' The agent was trying to make a plan. She couldn't involve other residents, ignorance was definitely bliss where they were concerned. She had to make contact with her office, praying that China's computer wasn't compromised and that Jan and his cronies hadn't yet realised they'd gone to China's apartment. The fire escape wasn't an option but that also meant Jan couldn't use it either.

China handed her laptop to the agent who took it to the writer's desk and began to type rapidly. 'Keep well away from the windows,' she said as China was drawn to the window. 'And the door, we can't trust it to withstand an assault.'

'An assault? You mean they'll break in here?' China's voice rose with her mounting fear.

'Don't know. Second thoughts, go to the door, quietly, and watch the hall through the spy-hole. Any movement, anything odd, let me know; *quietly*, understand?' Her fingers still speeding across the keys.

China moved to the door and placed her eye against the spy-hole. The hall was deserted. She kept turning to watch the agent, wondering what she was planning.

'Got some help coming, so we sit tight and wait,' Serra said eventually. Leaving the computer she pushed China aside so she could look through the spy-hole. 'Any chance some water?'

'Yeah, right away.' China moved to the kitchen, pushed a glass under the water tap on her ice-box and was about to return when she heard a loud thud and a muffled cry. She froze. She was about to ask Agent Serra if she was all right when a voice called out to her.

'China, get in here now.' It was Jan. How did he get in? She couldn't move, her legs felt like lead and she felt faint. 'Like now would be good,' he hissed. 'Don't make me come for you.'

Everything went black as terror streaked through her body, suffocating her, she couldn't hold on. The ground rose up, wobbled, and China felt herself falling, falling, falling...

Chapter Seven

'China, China, wake up, open your eyes.' Somewhere, distant and muffled, China could hear a voice. 'Wake up, you're all right, everything is all right.'

Gradually consciousness returned and she was able to open her eyes, bleary and unfocused. She shook her head, her thoughts muddy and confused. 'What?'

'You OK?'

'Who? What? Oh my god, Agent Serra, what happened?' She began recalling events, her heart pounded. She sat up, her head spinning, her eyes hurt. She rubbed them and stared at her companion, trying to focus. 'I thought Jan got in – where is he? I don't understand.'

'Agent who? What?' The girl laughed. 'Who the hell is Jan? There's no-one here, just you and me.'

'They rescued us, they saved us?'

'I have no idea what you're on about China, sit back and I'll bring you some water.'

'Yes, water, I remember, I was getting you some water and Jan got in! Are you all right? I don't understand, tell me.' China rubbed her head which was going to burst, confusion and fear filled her mind.

'Here drink this.'

China peered at her companion, recognition slowly dawning on her.

'You've been having a nightmare, screaming like a banshee when I was letting myself in – I could hear you all the way along the hall - I'm sure the whole building could hear you. I thought you were being murdered, you gave me such a fright I can tell you. I found you lying on the bed, thrashing around like crazy.' Her companion sat on the bed beside her. 'It's all right, you're safe. I'm here.'

'You! But you're...'

'Yes it's me, we were going for lunch, remember?'

'What? But you were, we were, I mean Jan, he was going to kill...'

'You've been dreaming, China, that's all. I don't know who your Jan is and what has been going on in that crazy head of yours, but I am real. There's no-one here but you and me and nobody's out to kill you.' She took the computer from the bed and placed it on her lap, tracing her finger across the pad, bringing up a Word document. She stooped to read the screen and laughed.

'You really are a case, China. You've been dreaming about your book. You must've fallen asleep writing last night. This is called Apartment 206c. You've written twelve chapters and you mention someone called Jan, oh, and you have me in it too, how exciting.'

'My book? But I thought, I mean it seemed so real...'

'You and your over-active imagination China, you're crazy, but so cool. I see I'm the heroine – that's good,' she laughed. 'I spend one night away and look at you, screaming and having nightmares fit to curdle anyone's blood, and you're not even ready – you're unbelievable.'

'Don't read any more, that's private until it's finished.' The author jumped off the bed and grabbed her laptop from her room-mate, Louise Serra. 'I remember now, I woke up early and decided to finish the chapter before getting up,' China said, still confused. 'I must've dropped off again.' Is that what happened, she wondered.

Louise laughed. 'Get ready, we're supposed to be having lunch with the girls remember? And if you don't get a move on, we'll be late as usual.' She took the glass back into the kitchen while China headed for the bathroom.

The doorbell rang. 'I'll get it,' Louise shouted, as she looked through the spy-hole. She put the chain on and opened it. 'Yes?'

'Hi, I'm your new neighbour, I heard screaming, so I thought I'd drop in and check everything's all right.' A tall, dark-haired young man with lightly tanned skin smiled at her.

'Who is it?' China appeared in her wrap, not yet ready for her shower. She gaped at the young man standing in her doorway.

'Hi guys, I'm Jan, your new neighbour in 206c.'

MURDER BY CHRISTMAS

Chapter One

The reading of Tiffany Blunt's Will was a subdued affair. Those who'd hoped to inherit didn't, and those who had been invited to attend without knowing why were suddenly beneficiaries. It was all a bit odd really.

'I know it's usual to invite only those named in the Will,' said Mr Lewis, Tiffany's solicitor, 'but this is an unusual situation. Ms Blunt's Will hasn't been what you'd call standard. I alone know what bequests she has made to charities and other organisations. As for other beneficiaries, I have been instructed to hand each of you a letter which contains her wishes. She asks that the contents of each of your letters is never revealed to each other or anyone else.'

Mr Lewis handed out three letters only. 'Even I don't know what is in them.'

The three not in receipt of a letter looked confused.

'Ah, Ms Blunt wanted you to be aware that she has excluded you from benefitting from her death because she felt that you had obtained enough from her during her lifetime.' His tone was stern as he looked at the two women and one man, over the top of his spectacles.

'She wanted you to be in no doubt that should you attempt to take steps to contest her wishes, any gifts she gave you in the past will be forfeit and passed to various charities as per her instructions to me.'

He polished his glasses and added, 'Ms Blunt died without having ever married and her estate is quite considerable. Her late fiancé, Malcolm Grant, died in a car accident on his stag night, just after his thirtieth birthday, having recently come into his late father's fortune.'

He looked around the room. 'The young man had only just made his Will it seems, naming Ms Blunt as sole beneficiary and this not six months after her uncle had died leaving her all his fortune too.' Those present exchanged looks wondering just how much she'd left.

The solicitor continued, 'I'm sure you know Ms Blunt was a frugal woman in many ways, not one to party or spend extravagantly.' He enjoyed seeing the look of greed on their faces. 'Therefore there is considerable wealth at stake.'

Actually, Tiffany Blunt outlived her fiancé by some twenty years, thus her bank account and shares in various successful corporations, both home and overseas, was more than considerable; Tiffany had been worth millions.

'I haven't had anything from her I didn't earn,' Tiffany's former house-keeper, Betty Green, muttered, 'but after almost twenty years faithful service, you'd think she'd have left me something; are you sure there's nothing?' she asked, staring at the letters the beneficiaries held excitedly. 'She used to say I would be able to have what I deserved in retirement, so I'm sure she'd have left me something.'

'She was explicit, Mrs Green. I cannot help you any further, good-day.'

Mr Lewis opened his office door for her and she reluctantly left, her face full of fury. She was glad she'd managed to take so many valuable things from her employer during her employment, not that they compensated for what she'd been led to expect. Well, Betty knew things about her former employer which she'd hinted she'd reveal if she was ever sacked, perhaps someone else would pay to keep them secret, she thought.

'I never asked for a penny and she was always generous to me, but she'd hinted more than once that I could expect....' David Sherman, her gardener of five years trailed off when the solicitor shook his head.

'Like I told Mrs Green, Ms Blunt's instructions are clear and non-negotiable. Sorry,' and he pointed to the door.

David Sherman's face was a picture of curiosity as he stared at the remaining people. He shrugged and left the room wondering what they would think if they knew about Tiffany and him.

'I know, I'm not entitled,' sighed Maddie Jones, Tiffany's secretary for ten years. 'But she promised me every time I asked for a raise. She said I'd get my reward when she died. Are you really sure she hasn't left me anything?'

Mr Lewis sighed loudly and opened the door for her. Maddie's expression was pinched as she swept past the other three. 'I could tell some tales,' she said angrily, 'and still might.'

Mr Lewis listened to her six-inch heels tapping along the parquet-floored corridor outside his offices, thinking she was a bad sort if ever there was one. He turned to the beneficiaries.

The three were wondering if there was anything else, anxious to get somewhere private to open their letters. The older man spoke first. 'I didn't really know Ms Blunt that well Mr Lewis. I'm surprised she'd leave me anything, after all, I was just her postman.'

46

'I'm sure she thought highly of you Mr Archer. I do hope you enjoy your bequest.' Mr Lewis showed the bewildered postman to the door. 'Remember, you must keep your bequest to yourself and never reveal it.'

Percy Archer nodded enthusiastically wondering how much she'd left him. He was a bachelor without any living relations and to those who were acquainted with him, via his rounds, he appeared to live a lonely life. Apart from a pint at the local pub on Saturday nights which he drank alone and in silence, he never mixed or appeared to have any friends. That might be changing now he'd come into a small fortune. Percy always dreamed of owning a car and going on holidays but he'd never been able to afford it. He whistled as he left the building, his step lighter.

Agatha Marshal fiddled with her envelope nervously. 'I'm so grateful to her Mr Lewis. I've never had much money but now I hope I'll be able to visit my sister in Canada.'

Tiffany often gave to the local Old Age Charity on whose behalf Ms Marshal collected money and other donated items; the only times they'd ever met. 'Oh, and of course I shall donate some to the charity I work for,' she added hastily.

'Ms Marshal, I am sure Ms Blunt was well aware just what her bequest will mean to you, indeed, to all of you.' He smiled thinly and pointed to the door. 'Goodbye Ms Marshal.'

The solicitor turned to the last person holding an envelope. 'Any questions Mr Seymour?'

Tim Seymour hesitated as if about to say something, but then changed his mind. 'No, I'm fine, thanks.' And the man who'd 'done something' for Tiffany twenty years ago left, wondering what had caused her to include him in her Will; they hadn't been in touch since the last time they'd met all those years ago, as agreed.

Mr Lewis read his own letter again. Tiffany had already made sure he was paid well for his services to her, which he'd carried out to the letter. However, he had one more service to discharge upon his deceased client's behalf. On Christmas Eve one of the beneficiaries – he had no idea who - would contact him, and he was to hand over a letter to them. His last act upon his client's behalf.

A few weeks more and Ms Blunt and her bequests would be his responsibility no longer. He could retire at last. He'd buy a yacht and sail away into retirement with his windfall.

Chapter Two

Percy Archer sat in The Jolly Farmer and stared at his letter, his breath rapid and shallow, his mind in turmoil. How did she know? What was he going to do? He'd never live it down. She couldn't really expect him to do it, could she? But what choice did he have?

Meanwhile, Agatha Marshal was having a similar experience in her kitchen where she held a damp cloth to her head, blood thumping through her temples. Dear God! Whatever am I going to do? She can't be serious? How could I? But Agatha knew that the alternative was unthinkable; she had her reputation after-all.

Tim Seymour read the letter twice more and then sighed. He knew this day would come eventually. He'd spent twenty years wondering if she would ever surface again. He'd only himself to blame, but he had been young and in love - desperate to have her at any cost. At any cost? She'd double-crossed him in the end. He wondered if he'd be able to do it again.

Chapter Three

Tiffany had been a watchful woman with a keen nose for mischief and intrigue. She didn't know what made her suspect the postman of hoarding the mail and not delivering every item entrusted to him by the Post Office. Little things just added up. He obviously wasn't spending any money he'd purloined on an extravagant lifestyle, so she doubted if he blackmailed people with the contents of their letters.

She couldn't resist herself; she had investigated and spied on Percy whenever she had the opportunity. It amused her. Percy Archer had another secret she soon discovered, one that wouldn't be well received in a rural community where the Church still played an important role in daily life; Percy's secret could ruin him. Tiffany relished the feeling of power this knowledge gave her. She bided her time just knowing it would come in handy one day.

Percy had no idea anyone had rumbled his thefts. The Post Office was in such a shambles these days, it was easy to 'miss-lay' the odd delivery or sack. He couldn't help himself. He'd read that stress can make you do all sorts of weird stuff, so he put it down to stress. His secret life was taking its toll on him he knew, yet his 'non-deliveries,' afforded some relief, though he couldn't explain why.

Now it was all coming to a head and if he didn't do as she asked he'd have to face the music and the humiliation of not just being labelled a thief and possibly going to prison, but the whole village would find out that he was a cross-dresser. He was on the Church Finance Committee for goodness sakes. He couldn't stand it. He'd do anything to keep his secret, but Ms Blunt asked too much.

Percy rushed out of the pub and went home where he found solace in putting his late mother's clothes and make-up on, before making himself a stiff drink.

*****

Agatha paced back and forth, reading her letter over and over. If this got out she'd be ruined. Her plans to sit on the Parish Council would be finished and she'd have to resign from the Funding Committee for the new church roof. Then there was the charity; what if they pressed charges? She might end up in prison; ruined. How did Tiffany find out? What was she to do? Agatha was sure she hadn't the stomach for what Tiffany asked; had she?

The disappointment felt by Percy and Agatha at not being able to obtain any financial reward from Tiffany unless they carried out their given tasks, without question, and without telling another living soul, was acute. Substantial amounts were at stake and within their grasp, but both would-be beneficiaries were in a quandary; Tiffany asked the unthinkable.

*****

Tim sipped his scotch and thought about Tiffany and what he'd done for her all those years ago, and how she'd betrayed him and blackmailed him into silence. Now she wanted him to do it again. He wished there was a way, but deep down he knew there wasn't; he had to carry out her wishes, there was too much at stake. Yet inheriting her money was not an incentive - his life and freedom was.

Tim thought about his task. It shouldn't be too difficult to execute. He needed to watch events unfolding in the village before he could act, anyway. All he had to do was plan and wait. He poured another scotch and considered the matter further.

Chapter Four

After the initial shock Percy calmed down and began to think about his task. Actually, it might not be so terrible or difficult after-all. The woman was a pest, into everyone's business as he'd discovered when he'd read a letter from a local solicitor threatening legal action if she continued to slander a respected local doctor. It was one of a few he'd opened when he first started to 'caretake' the mail he failed to deliver.

Percy recalled the extent of Betty Green's blackmail throughout the village; he'd be doing a public service come to think of it, preventing her 'career' from progressing any further. He resolved to accept Ms Blunt's task and dressed in his beloved mother's clothes once more. He watched himself in her dressing room mirror as he considered ways and means.

Agatha was unable to sleep for worry. She tossed and turned, battling with the demons Ms Blunt had visited upon her. There was no way round it that she could see. She'd have to go public about her youthful mistake and subsequent light-fingered moment, the alternative was too awful, but then there was the money. It was enough to drive a woman to drink.

Agatha had lived with the shame of her fall from grace for many years. She'd only ever done it once in her whole life and being unmarried she'd made her decision at a time when such things were barely legal. How did Tiffany find out? It was the only time she'd ever stolen anything in her life and desperation drove her to do it; stealing the money from work to pay for the abortion. She'd spent her life trying to make amends ever since. Now this. Her reputation was everything to her. She'd do what she was asked.

*****

Percy Archer was acquainted with Mrs Green but only on nodding terms, passing the time of day when he delivered mail for Ms Blunt or to Mrs Green herself. He began to watch her closely, taking more of a keen interest in her than before. Now that her employer was dead she'd managed to obtain work in several households on a part-time basis, affording her more opportunities to steal and to delve into her unsuspecting and trusting employers' lives. Percy noticed she'd go into the nearby town once a week, on the train, to visit the antique shops. Always with something to sell. Then she'd make her way to one of the local building societies where she'd make a deposit.

After a couple of weeks Percy's plan was beginning to form. He could do as Ms Blunt asked and he was certain he'd get away with it.

Agatha Marshal's terror finally persuaded her. She'd no choice really and besides she didn't like the jumped up little madam one bit. In fact, she thought of her as a bit of a tart and was really surprised that Ms Blunt ever employed her in the first place. The more Agatha thought about it the more she convinced herself she'd be doing society a favour.

Maddie Jones lived her immoral life on the same street as Agatha, a few doors down opposite the Post Office, and so it wasn't hard to keep an eye on her and her movements. Maddie didn't have one boyfriend, she had several - if you could call them that. Most were older men, business types from what Agatha deduced, most likely able to spend a fortune on the little money-grabber; payment in kind more like. Agatha assumed most were probably married and having a bit on the side.

One in particular stood out, a man in his early fifties who drove a blue Mercedes convertible. Agatha soon discovered that Maddie was not just working for him as his *'Personal Assistant.'* She'd laughed out loud when she'd found out what sort of *'assistance'* Maddie offered him personally.

Agatha was amazed to see a lorry pull up outside Maddie's terraced house one day and watched in fascination as what looked like a home gym was unloaded and taken into the house. She knew the girl was a member of the local Aerobics and Pilates group which met in the village hall weekly – Agatha had toyed with the idea of joining at one time but the sight of all those young things with perfect physiques prancing around in next to nothing had put her off. She wondered why Maddie was having a gym installed at home, but it gave her an idea.

*****

Tim kept an eye on Percy and Agatha. He was sure they'd been given tasks to perform in return for Tiffany's money. He hardly knew them except by sight. Keeping a low profile so they wouldn't spot his interest in them was difficult. The other person of interest, as per his instructions, was David Sherman. Tim soon discovered that he was a part-time gardener for several of the larger houses just outside the village. David also had an allotment of his own on the edge of the village where he spent most of his spare time when he wasn't tending to a few of his female client's and their *'bedding problems.'*

The allotment afforded no end of possibilities.

Chapter Five

Betty Green counted the money she'd earned from the sale of a silver Georgian teapot and stand which she'd 'acquired,' from Mrs Cuthbert, widow of the Major who'd once rode to hounds and who'd died falling off of his horse when hunt protestors had startled his mount as they crossed a stream in the local farmer's field.

Mrs Cuthbert was losing the plot and half the time didn't know what day of the week it was. At one time Betty was able to obtain regular *'financial contributions'* from the woman whose secrets she'd discovered whilst working for her some time before her employer started to lose her memory. Later, as Mrs Cuthbert's dementia progressed she'd mistaken Betty for her long-lost sister many a time, which suited Betty just fine.

'Martha, dear, I've found you the most wonderful birthday gift. I haven't had time to wrap it, I do hope you like it,' she'd said to Betty recently.

'Oh, thank you, dear sister,' Betty said, going along with the confused woman. Never one to look a gift horse in the mouth. The silverware was worth a considerable sum and Betty was anxious to get to the antique shop and building society before closing time.

*****

Standing on the platform waiting for the train back to the village, Betty was deep in thought about her bank account and the growing sums in it. Being Saturday the station platform was crowded with football fans on their way to see their local team play away. Spirits were high as they sang and chanted, waving their scarves and tins of lager. Betty hardly noticed them milling around her as she planned how she'd get her hands on a lovely little silver snuff box she'd seen on the dressing table of one of her 'clients'.

The through train to London was due in first. Betty didn't know what hit her as she fell off the platform and into its path. A gentle shove in the small of her back was all it took.

Percy disappeared into the crowds as they rushed to the edge of the platform to gawk at what was left of Betty after the high-speed train had disappeared into the distance, its driver possibly unaware of the accident. But, in any case, even if he had been it would've taken some time to stop and by that time Percy would be on his bike half-way home. He shook from head to foot as he pedalled, hardly able to believe what he'd just done.

'I'll have a double on the rocks please.' His first port of call was the pub where he planned on calming his nerves for the rest of the afternoon.

Tim saw Percy leaving the station just as an announcement came over the PA system.

'Due to an incident on the line all trains have been cancelled until further notice'.

He'd seen them both enter the station shortly before. Betty seemed unaware of Percy as she waited at the ticket office. Tim watched from just outside the entrance wondering why Percy hid behind the newspaper stand, lingering there until the train was imminent when he disappeared towards the platform.

Cries of horror and shock alerted Tim that something had happened, not to mention the sight of a guilty looking Percy hurrying away in the opposite direction to everyone else. Tim didn't need sixth sense to work out what.

He left the station quickly before the police and ambulance arrived wondering why Tiffany wanted Betty Green bumped off.

How clever, he thought, Tiffany had somehow managed to force Percy into doing her bidding. But why? He was going to have to keep a closer eye on the others.

*****

Days passed with Percy beside himself with worry waiting for the knock on the door. But it didn't come. He watched all the news bulletins waiting for some clue as to what the police were doing.

So far it seemed that Betty's death was being treated as an accident; she'd been standing too close to the edge of the platform and with so many people jostling around it was possible someone knocked into her accidentally - nothing had shown up on the CCTV footage to make them think otherwise.

Percy had got away with it. He didn't feel at all happy about it and reading his letter again with instructions as to how he'd obtain Tiffany's bequest of £2,000,000, didn't ease his conscience. He was dressing in Mother's clothes more frequently and had given notice at work, relief building as he prepared to leave his old life behind.

A week later Percy boarded a British Airways flight for his all-expenses-paid round the world trip, his tickets and generous spending money having arrived as per his letter, along with details of a bank account in his name, in Mauritius, his first destination.

He doubted he'd ever return to England and from now on he'd wear whatever he liked.

Chapter Six

Agatha knocked on Maddie's door careful to ensure no-one was about. Luckily the street lamp opposite was out of order so she was well hidden in the depths of the outside porch. Maddie's hall light went on and her shadow advanced towards the partially glazed front door,

'Yes, hello, who is it?'

Agatha almost whispered through the door, 'it's Agatha Marshal, you'll remember me from the reading of Ms Blunt's Will.'

'Oh, hello Ms Marshal, excuse my get-up, I've been trying out my new home gym.' Maddie opened the door only a fraction but Agatha quickly registered what she was wearing.

She was reminded of a TV Breakfast show of years gone by as 'The Green Goddess' came to mind.

'Oh how exciting, I'm sorry to interrupt you my dear but I won't keep you long.' Her smile full of concern. 'Can't have you catching your death after your work-out can we?' She smiled again, 'perhaps I'd better come in for a moment; it's really cold out here.'

Maddie hesitated briefly and then took the door off the chain and ushered Agatha inside.

'What can I do for you, Ms Marshal?' Maddie wiped herself down with a towel and kept running on the spot slowly so as not to stiffen up after her work-out.

'It might be best if you continue with your exercise whilst we chat,' Agatha suggested. She wanted Maddie to show her the gym which she'd seen her using in the front upstairs bedroom. 'Saves you getting chilled, besides, I've always been fascinated by gym equipment.'

She moved towards the stairs. 'I'd love to see it. I had one of those vibrating belts once - you know - the ones which were supposed to jiggle your fat away.' Agatha laughed. 'As you can see, Maddie, it didn't work for me.'

'Oh, yes, by all means, do come up.' And Maddie led the way upstairs. 'I've almost finished. I've got one of those programmes on my tablet which I follow and I don't want to get behind in points.'

Agatha followed her into quite a large room with all manner of gym equipment installed, complete with mirrored walls. 'Personal assistance' really does pay well, Agatha thought, as she looked around. She'd read somewhere that floors had to be re-enforced to take the weight of gym equipment.

'Do take a seat, Ms Marshal.' Maddie pointed to a work-out bench. 'Won't be a minute and then we can chat.'

Maddie straddled a long bench with weights after making some adjustments. For a few moments Maddie lifted weights, panting as she worked. Agatha watched feeling detached and not a bit nervous, which really surprised her. This was going better than she could've imagined. She kept her coat and gloves on even though the room felt a little stuffy. Maddie didn't seem to mind the airless room.

'I thought you had to have someone standing behind you, in case of an accident.' Agatha walked over to Maddie who was covered in perspiration.

'I know but I'm fine Ms Marshal, I've not increased the weights for some time so I'm not pushing myself, though I could of course.'

Agatha stood behind Maddie smiling down at her. 'You're so strong I'm really impressed. When do you think you'll manage to increase the weights?' Agatha inspected the contraption carefully. 'Though I suppose you can't really manage anything heavier, you're such a slight little thing,' tempted Agatha, a devious glint in her eyes. Maddie was a vain young woman and Agatha waited for her to take the bait.

Maddie paused and then stood up, removing the weight. She picked up the next heaviest weight and placed it on the contraption, ready.

'Ms Marshal, do you mind remaining where you are as I lift this? It's heavier and I've only tried it once before, but I can do it.'

Agatha smiled, 'of course, my dear, don't worry. I'll be right behind you.'

Maddie raised the weight, closing her eyes in concentration. Just as she extended her arms fully Agatha leaned over the girl and tickled her under her arms. It had the desired effect. Maddie dropped the weight in shock and it landed on her throat.

Agatha felt for a pulse but there wasn't one and with a quick glance around the room she made her way back downstairs, satisfied she'd touched nothing whilst in the house. She manipulated the front door latch with one of Maddie's scarves which was hanging on a coat peg nearby, dropping it inside the door as she closed it. She stood for a few moments looking about her in the gloom. The street was deserted and the houses opposite had already drawn their curtains against the cold winter evening.

Satisfied with herself, yet amazed at her ability to do something so unimaginably wicked, Agatha made her way home, making plans for her windfall. Soon she'd be on a world cruise, all expenses paid, stopping off in the Cayman Islands where a bank account bore her name with £2,000,000 credited. She'd never return to England. A world where she could be herself, free from shame, awaited her. She even forgot to donate to charity as promised.

*****

Tim had watched Agatha Marshal as she left Maddie's house, intrigued as to what she'd been up to. The woman had behaved furtively and Tim was certain that Agatha had carried out Tiffany's instructions which, he was now convinced, involved murdering those at the reading of her Will who hadn't benefitted.

He felt a brief twinge of conscience as he wondered if he should've warned the young woman, but until he'd watched Agatha's exit he'd not been sure of his suspicions. In any case, he had his own instructions to follow and upsetting Tiffany's plans might cause him problems in the end. It would soon be time for him to act.

*****

Maddie's death was investigated and just like Betty's the same conclusion was reached; accidental death. The local Press ran a series of articles warning of the dangers of keep fit and exercising alone and another about standing too close to the edge on railway platforms. No link between the two women was made.

Both Agatha and Percy's properties were put up for sale, all enquires to go through Mr Lewis, solicitor. Local gossip concluded they'd run off together after conducting a secret affair for decades.

Chapter Seven

Tim kept a watchful eye in-case Tiffany had someone unknown tasked with his demise. So far nothing gave him cause for suspicion as he set about his own tasks with a heavy heart. He just wanted it all to be over.

David Sherman's gardening skills had provided him with an impressive customer base Tim observed over a number of weeks, the majority of whom were women of a 'certain age' with considerable disposable income. Tiffany appeared to have been a regular too.

A search of his home afforded him the reason for David's success with his 'ladies.' Not only was David a superb gardener but he provided 'extras' for his clients; at a price. Tim picked up on local gossip and had soon cottoned on to the sexual extras the handsome young man provided for these bored, lonely, married women. But it was David's other 'extras' which now interested Tim, as he observed his target's daily life. David also supplied Cocaine to some of his clients – which got Tim's imagination working over-time.

The young gardener was very lax when it came to keeping his poisons and pesticides under lock and key. Most times his greenhouses and shed on his allotment - behind his former farm cottage on the edge of the village - were left unlocked without any visible means of alarm or precautions to prevent theft.

Wednesday afternoon's David regularly worked in the largest garden on the far side of the village belonging to a wealthy widow who normally occupied his talents, not just in her numerous flower beds, but in her comfy queen-sized bed too. Tim observed that David could be relied upon to be away from his cottage for several hours. Plenty of time for him to have a thorough examination of the premises enabling him to put his plan into action.

Tim soon observed that David liked his drink; his kitchen cabinets held several bottles of various spirits. A half-full bottle of vodka beside a plain glass bottle of what, Tim assumed, was tonic water or lemonade – also about half full - was on the kitchen dresser beside a large glass tumbler. Wearing gloves Tim sniffed the contents of each, and tipping a little liquid on to a spoon he found in the dresser drawer, took a sip; one bottle contained Vodka, the other lemonade - sweet tasting - possibly home-made. He washed the spoon and returned it to the drawer.

A search of the greenhouse afforded nothing much of use to Tim. Various insecticides gave him food for thought, but he soon dismissed them. He wanted David's death to be sudden and plausible.

Tim rummaged around carefully without leaving any trace of his search. He stepped on a loose floorboard inside the shed which, when pulled up, revealed the gardener's stash of the drugs he sold to his customers and which Tim had observed him using himself, more than once, when he'd observed him through his sitting room windows, late evenings.

He thought about doctoring the drugs but decided against it. Several empty glass bottles similar to the one containing lemonade lined the shelves inside the shed, next to other bottles containing a clear liquid. When unscrewed he noticed one didn't have much of an odour and the other smelled of turpentine. He replaced the tops. Bending down Tim opened a similar bottle, sniffed, and replaced the top. He removed the bottle of clear liquid from underneath the workbench.

Chapter Eight

A week later David set off for his regular Wednesday appointment with his customer, observed by Tim. When he was sure the gardener wouldn't return for some time Tim made a quick visit to the gigolo's home. He'd switched his mobile off and removed the sim card and battery before leaving his own home; he didn't want anyone triangulating his location if anything went wrong.

David had a new bottle of lemonade on the dresser much to Tim's relief when he went into the kitchen. Wearing surgical gloves he tipped some lemonade on the flower bed at the back of the cottage, making sure he hadn't left any footprints in the garden or in the kitchen when he returned to add a quantity of methanol to the remaining lemonade, using a small funnel to transfer the colourless liquid. He placed the funnel in a ziploc bag which he'd dispose of later on his walk home, along with the gloves.

Returning to the shed Tim placed the bottle of methanol on the shelf next to the remaining lemonade bottles and he placed the turpentine next to that. He checked he'd left no tell-tale dust rings where he'd removed the bottles and, after a quick look round to ensure he'd left nothing to show his presence there, walked the half mile back down the lane, across the fields towards The Jolly Farmer where he'd ordered lunch, checking his surroundings as he went.

He didn't spy a soul on his way as he disposed of the ziploc bag. Tim replaced everything he'd removed from his mobile, switching it back on once inside the pub.

*****

After lunch, Tim settled by the open fire in the snug to read the latest David Baldacci novel he had with him. Later he had a few drinks, making small talk with whoever he could find in the saloon bar before heading back to the flat he'd recently rented, to watch his new boxed set of Game of Thrones.

At 9 pm Tim telephoned his landlord from his mobile to complain his hot water boiler was not working properly; the GPS setting his location and time. There was nothing to ever link him to David in the event of his death being considered suspicious. Methanol could take between 12-24 hours to work and Tim planned to make his whereabouts known to as many people as he could during this time. David could be anywhere when he went into a coma and death struck.

The local Press ran a front-page article about the dangers of putting lethal house-hold products in unlabelled bottles similar to those holding soft drinks and water, following the tragic accidental death of a young man who'd muddled his lemonade bottle with one containing methanol, stored carelessly in his garden shed. David had also consumed Cocaine prior to his demise.

Tim read the news online, listened to the local radio and television news but apart from reporting the tragic loss of a highly popular young gardener briefly, David was soon forgotten when the media moved on to the imminent arrival of 50 unaccompanied male Syrian teenagers from Calais.

Chapter Nine

On Christmas Eve Tim arrived late at Mr Lewis' offices as instructed. His flat vacated, his few personal chores dealt with, he was ready to disappear into the vastness of Indonesia once more, free of Tiffany. A tree with decorations stood in one corner of reception, lights blinking on and off, festive cards and bunting dangled from the ceiling. Christmas, thought Tim, what a flipping joke.

Lewis was alone in his office, his staff having left at lunchtime. He'd used his time gathering all his remaining paperwork, files, and company computer technology together, thus ensuring any record of his recent activities on behalf of Ms Blunt had been removed. He loaded everything into his car. He'd been systematically erasing himself from her business at the firm for the last few weeks, as per her instructions. There was nothing left now. No trace of his services on Tiffany's behalf. At last he could retire. He'd always wanted to visit Kathmandu and immerse himself in the beauty and culture of the mountains.

'Ah! I've been expecting you, please sit down.' Mr Lewis stood behind his desk, somehow unsurprised Seymour would be the one beneficiary remaining. 'Anyone see you come in?'

'Thanks,' Tim shook his head, sitting down cautiously. 'No-one about. Too cold out there,' he said as he noticed the solicitor eyeing his leather gloves, not without some suspicion in his eyes.

*****

Mr Lewis sat down regarding Tim over the top of his spectacles, wary. 'Can I offer you a festive drink? There's only a little scotch and vodka with mixers. The girls saw most of it off this morning before breaking up for the holidays.'

'No, no worries.' Tim didn't trust Lewis one bit. He'd observed the solicitor for the past few weeks, watching him removing items from his offices and his home late at night. Did Lewis have a task to perform?

'Coffee, tea?' Lewis' mind raced, he wanted to get away. 'Something to warm you up?' The deaths of Tiffany's beneficiaries hadn't gone unnoticed by him. Co-incidences didn't happen. He was fearful of his guest.

Tim shook his head. No way, he thought. He didn't trust the solicitor.

'You've completed the tasks according to your instructions?'

Tim nodded, aware that he might be recorded. He glanced around wondering if there was any CCTV or hidden camera he should deal with, any voice recording devices.

'If it's all the same to you, I'd like to discuss anything further outside.' Tim stood and moved towards the door.

'Why? It's freezing out there.' Lewis realised the streets were deserted, too cold for even foxes to venture out seeking food.

He reluctantly followed Tim into reception, anxiety seeping through every pore. He didn't want to be alone with the man without witnesses. 'I don't understand, what's wrong with my office?'

'Is there another office on this floor we can use?' Tim left reception and Lewis followed.

'Well, not open. On the top floor there's a conference room, I haven't locked up yet so it should be open,' Lewis suggested, heart pounding with fear. It's not how it's supposed to go, he thought. 'Can't we stay in the hall?'

'I would prefer the conference room. Is there any heating up there? I'm frozen.' Tim waited as a worried looking Lewis guided him towards the lift. 'No lifts, can't stand them.'

Lewis walked to the end of the corridor and led the way up several flights of stairs to the conference room. He held the door open for Tim.

*****

The solicitor handed Tim a sealed envelope written in Tiffany's own hand, addressed to 'The Last Beneficiary.'

'I've no idea of the contents. As you can see she has placed a wax seal on it similar to the letters the other beneficiaries received.'

Tim looked at it and decided he'd open it later. 'Thanks.' He put it in his jacket pocket.

'Well, that is all I think so I'll bid you goodnight and Happy Christmas,' Lewis said, anxious to leave the top floor and be on his way to his new yacht moored in a little bay on the coast of Cornwall. He planned a short holiday sailing around the Med before flying to India and then on to Nepal and obscurity.

'Did you know Tiffany well?' Tim asked, watching Lewis creep towards the door.

'My father was Chief Constable in this area when she was young, our families – parents - were close. One of my father's cousins was her family solicitor and took me into practice with him. When he died I inherited the company and Tiffany. I didn't know her that well, however.' Lewis stopped. 'Why do you ask?'

'Do you have any idea what's been happening Mr Lewis, what her requests were?' Tim watched the nervous solicitor carefully. 'You ensured all the money was paid out and that those receiving it could leave their present lives behind and disappear. Did you ever ask her why?'

'Ms Blunt dealt with the details herself. I didn't see the contents of the letters and all I had to do was distribute them after reading her Will. Which I've done. I know nothing of what the beneficiaries' did to deserve their good fortune. I don't want to know. I don't know what you or anyone else had to do for her. She once told me she'd deep affection for you - when I was adding you to her Will - and that you'd done her a great service which she was rewarding.'

Tim laughed heartily. 'Rewarding.'

'Yes, well, if that is all I'll be off now.' Lewis almost ran from the room. Tim didn't follow, he was too weary.

Poor Lewis. He was about to get this reward too.

Chapter Ten

Tim read the reports of the explosion aboard *My Dream* with a mixture of sadness and relief. A tragic accident according to the Press. There was a fuel leak and Mr Lewis must've lit his cigar and up it all went. The final part of his plan had fallen into place. He could relax for the first time in years.

It was Boxing Day and Tim was sitting in the VIP lounge at Heathrow waiting for his flight to be called. Christmas songs played endlessly on a loop as he waited. After he'd read his bequest described in Tiffany's first letter following the Will reading, he'd destroyed it as instructed. He too wanted a new life and grasped at the straw she offered him.

She'd expressed sorrow she'd blackmailed him into keeping silent about the murder of her fiancé all these years – Tim snorted, yeah right – but she had no choice. Tim recalled being so in love he'd agreed to take the blame, if any should be attributed, for her fiancé's death. So smitten was he.

He even helped cover up the murder of her uncle which initially he'd thought was an accident until she inherited everything he had. By then it was too late. She'd manufactured and hidden evidence which implicated Tim in both murders, holding it over him all these years, buying his silence.

He had been glad to get away from her, to forget it all. He knew she had someone tame high up in the police who'd be given the evidence if he went back on anything and he wasn't stupid. His word against hers, plus the evidence. No; he was her *patsy.* Apparently the solicitor's father was the tame copper.

He'd opened the second letter Tiffany left for him soon after he left the solicitor's freezing office. Tiffany had been confident that David would be the sole surviving beneficiary.

Tiffany regretted her deeds and wanted to make it up to him but first she wanted to ensure he'd carry out a few more tasks to guarantee his complete and utter silence forever. Why she cared what anyone would think after her death, he couldn't imagine. But she did.

True to the woman he'd come to know and hate she wanted to ensure that some old scores were settled. Betty had robbed her, Maddie had tried to blackmail her, and David had cheated on her and sold drugs to anyone he could. She hated anything to do with drugs. She'd apparently felt sorry for Percy and Agatha and their sad lives. However, it didn't stop her using them as her tools of revenge - as she'd used Tim once again. What a twisted woman she was.

When Tim arrived at Mr Lewis' offices the solicitor had already disposed of all papers and other materials left with him as instructed. Lewis knew not what they were or contained and didn't want to. Lewis was to destroy everything only when he'd learned of the death of David Sherman.

Tiffany had kept her word and all evidence implicating Tim in any past murders had been sent to him by courier in a sealed box Christmas night, which Tim destroyed following his final task; the one last deed Tim had to carry out to secure his continued freedom. He'd never hesitated really - he knew he'd do it. He was a coward.

Before Christmas day was over - Tiffany's birthday - one way or another Mr Lewis, the last pawn in her evil plan, had to be disposed of. Only then would Tim be able to get on with his life. Now he had enough money to last a lifetime, no links or ties to the past.

No more Tiffany. No more blackmail. Percy was free, Agatha was free. Everyone was free because they'd all committed murder by Christmas

THE WATCHERS

Chapter One

As if stuck with super-glue her hand held fast to the receiver. The phone rang again and again yet still she could not move. Her knuckles ached from gripping it. She willed it to stop, yet somewhere inside her mind she wanted to answer it, to put herself out of her misery - she knew it was him again.

'Oh God, please make it stop, make him go away,' she whispered.

Candice held her breath. Her heart was making her blouse shake as it thudded faster and faster. Sweat ran down between her breasts and her legs felt as if they were going to give from under her. The constant ringing vibrated through her hand and up her arm. Mesmerised she suddenly found herself humming the ABBA song with *Ring, Ring, Ring,* in the lyrics and she almost giggled. It stopped. Silence.

She shook her head in disbelief and then tried to remove her hand from the receiver but her fingers had seized around it and the pain moving them soon brought her back to reality. She steadied herself against the cold smooth hall wall and tried to pace her breaths so that her light-headedness began to lift.

'Thank you, God,' she said aloud.

Eventually, she managed to go into the kitchen. In the cupboard by the fridge she found an opened bottle of wine left over from last night. Grabbing a mug from the drainer she poured the remainder of the wine into it and almost threw it down her throat. Closing her eyes as the smooth liquid gushed into her she began to feel calmer. She finished the last drops, licking her lips. Taking huge deep breaths in through her nose and out through her mouth: in and out, in and out, slowly, she tried to centre herself.

'Pull yourself together, silly bitch,' she told herself.

Candice struggled with what to do. Her thoughts were always about the same thing these days. She had no-one to turn to and when it first happened she'd dismissed it as a crank call. But night after night the calls came. For over two months she had dreaded nine o'clock and she'd started watching the clock as the minutes ticked nearer to it every evening when she got in from work.

At first she was so terrified she wasn't even sure it was a man's voice. But later she forced herself to listen properly and after a few weeks she even started to think she knew who it was. It was the postman. No, it was the guy from the corner shop, or was it the bloke who had done her MOT? She dismissed these thoughts in the end telling herself she was too stressed to really be sure of anything. It could be anyone, perhaps someone she'd never met.

Chapter Two

From the moment she woke from her restless sleep where she dreamed of headless men chasing her down dark alley-ways, until she laid her drink fuddled head on the pillow at night in the hope that alcohol would wipe her brain clean so she could sleep, her thoughts were always of him. Him. Whoever 'him' was.

Candice was driving herself nuts trying to find out who was doing this to her. She couldn't think of anyone she'd upset that badly they'd want to terrorise her like this. Apart from people at work she kept herself to herself and rarely went out socially preferring her own company since she split from Ollie a year ago.

'No, he couldn't,' she kept telling herself whenever she wondered if he was capable of such nastiness towards her.

Concentration on anything was virtually impossible lately and trying to work out who and why and what to do was getting harder and harder, the more frightened and stressed she became. Once she'd walked up to a parked police car and was about to ask for help having stood watching the occupants eating their lunch for a good ten minutes before she summoned the courage but, just as she was about to tap on the window, they started the car and shot off down the high street with lights flashing and siren blaring. She couldn't bring herself try again.

Every time she left the house she checked to see if anyone was lurking or looking suspicious before setting foot outside. She was becoming paranoid about being followed and being watched but so far there wasn't any evidence of anyone taking more than a fleeting interest in her. Except once that is. She nearly got into a bit of a ding-dong at the bus stop with a young lad who kept looking at her and smiling.

'What're you staring at?' she'd hissed at him, 'lost your book of animals or something?' And when she actually raised her brolly at him the poor chap fell in the road trying to get out of her way.

'Sorry, I thought I knew you,' he shouted above the traffic noise. 'You look like one of my sister's old schoolmates. My mistake, sorry.'

He stepped back on the pavement but kept his distance from her. Candice eyed him suspiciously. She couldn't place him as an old school mate's brother.

'Yeah well, it's rude to stare and I've never seen you before so I doubt I knew your sister, if you've got one that is.'

He seemed relieved when the bus arrived soon after and went upstairs when he'd got his ticket.

The phone rang again. Candice almost dropped her mug. She bolted out of her seat, panic rising in her chest again, her blood rushing to her head. She looked at the clock and immediately remembered she was expecting a call from a colleague at work.

'Candice, hi it's me, Jane, did you find out if you could cover for me tomorrow?' Jane's call was dead on time as arranged.

'Oh, Jane, sorry I was miles away. Yep, I checked my diary and I can do it for you. No problem.' Candice tried to sound normal but she knew her voice was shaking, 'what time do you have your scan?'

'My appointment is for nine in the morning, so I'll need to be there a bit before. I really appreciate it and I'll do the same for you, if ever.' The office ran on flexi-time as long as there was always someone to cover the reception desk early mornings. Jane was the only receptionist since the cut-backs so everyone had to muck in if ever she wasn't there.

'Don't worry, I'll be in early and put the phones and coffee machine on.'

'All right. I'll see you later in the morning when I get back, thanks so much.'

'Hope it goes well for you. See you after, bye,' and she hung up aware that she had been standing on tiptoe throughout the conversation, her body rigid.

Chapter Three

Across the road and out of view a figure lurked in the shadows waiting for the bedroom light to go on. He gazed at the house mindful of the passing traffic going about its business. Drivers and pedestrians oblivious to him standing there - thrilled at the thought of being an invisible presence - watching.

Night after night he took up the same position where he could see the house and what was happening inside. But most of all he could see her. She always left it until it got dark to close her curtains and when she was going upstairs he could see her clearly through the curtain-less landing window. He watched her going back and forth on the landing between rooms, sometimes in her dressing gown. He'd get a fleeting glimpse as she moved into her bedroom before she closed the curtains. Her watcher never tired of the spectacle which he knew was put on just for him.

*****

Just as Candice was getting into bed a car passed by slowly, headlights dimmed and its occupant difficult to see. His turned-up jacket collar almost covered his face and his baseball cap was pulled down low. As the car entered her street the man in the shadows moved further into the gloom, puzzled. He was sure the car had passed by twice before, moving slowly as it passed the house.

'Unmarked police car?' he muttered, venturing a little way out of the shadows to peer after it as it disappeared from sight. Perhaps she'd squealed. He thrilled at the thought of her terror yet was nervous she might have called the police. Would it return again he wondered? Pressing the screen on his mobile he checked the time. Best keep an eye on the time and see if a routine emerged; police kept to routines.

Oblivious of her watchers Candice got into bed with her third glass of wine and reached for her novel. Perhaps Kathy Reichs would take her mind off her own fear. She'd unplugged the land-line and put her mobile on vibrate; so far he hadn't called her on that. It seemed the only way to get even a few hours' sleep these days was in the glass she held. She knew it wouldn't solve her problems but it did steady her nerves. Alcohol was the only way she'd get any sleep, any peace. Luckily she never seemed to suffer from hangovers, even after drinking a whole bottle.

She bolted upright, heart and head pounding. Her book had fallen to the floor and at first she thought that was what had woken her. She leaned down to pick it up almost falling out of bed when she heard the commotion. Sitting up again she tilted her head straining to hear where the muffled sounds were coming from.

Men's voices raised in anger drifted up from the street outside.

Candice swung her legs out of bed, her feet found her slippers and grabbing her dressing gown she switched off her bedside lamp before moving carefully to her window. Brushing the curtain aside her eyes took a moment to adjust to the street lighting and for a few seconds she couldn't see anything as she scanned the street.

A movement across the road by the hedge, outside the bungalow where the old man who'd lost a leg in WW2 lived, caught her attention. It couldn't be him, she thought, he rarely came outside and certainly not at this time of night in his wheelchair.

'Who the hell would be lurking about outside at this time of night?' Candice asked out loud.

What am I like these days, she thought. Always talking out loud to myself. I'm losing it big time.

She squinted, her nose up against the glass, and thought she saw some movement between the hedge and a parked car. Bloody car thieves, joy riders about to pinch the car she decided and quietly opened the window ready to give them a piece of her mind. But then she realised there were two figures who appeared to be dancing back and forth, apparently not interested in the car. A courting couple? She didn't think so. She was sure she could hear male voices and she realised they were arguing, their tone angry, but trying to keep the noise down as they argued. There was definitely something odd about their movements too. Were they actually fighting?

Candice leaned out as far as she dared mindful she could fall and watched the two shadowy figures lunging at each other, ducking and diving. Two men were fighting – she wasn't mistaken. Now her eyes were fully adjusted she could see them clearly in the lamplight. One was tall and big built and the other was smaller, slender, and possibly younger, but she couldn't be sure. Candice couldn't make out their features.

Well, I never! She'd never seen anything like it in this street before, perhaps a couple of miles away on the Council estate people would see this sort of thing, but this was a respectable neighbourhood, housing professionals who owned their own homes. Nothing exciting ever happened unless you counted New Year's Eve about two years ago when the couple three doors up had a party which got out of hand and someone called the police, but that was over before she'd even realised anything was going on. She'd heard the music but not much else.

Chapter Four

The men's grunts filled the air, their breath coming in short bursts, wafting off like smoke signals into the cold night. Candice looked to see if anyone else had been woken by their struggles, but she couldn't see anyone; the neighbours' lights were off. The traffic had stopped cutting through to the main road, so she knew it must be quite late.

Candice considered shouting to them or calling the police but something stopped her. Despite her abhorrence of violence, she was fascinated. It occurred to her this wasn't a drunken fight or a falling out of friends. There was a sinister quality about it she felt; a fight to the end. She watched enthralled, the cold night air giving her goose bumps. She saw her own breath floating off into the night just before the moon went behind a cloud.

Back and forth the shadows moved, sometimes one falling down only to struggle up again, and then the other would take a stomach or head blow and he'd fall. Their grunts reminded her of Bill Odie's TV wildlife show and the rutting deer on one of the Scottish Islands which the programme featured every year. They often fought until the death. She shuddered at the thought. Surely not!

The moon appeared again just as one of the figures, the smaller one, fell to the ground and cried out in pain. The taller man stooped over him, his hands on his knees, gasping.

He bent lower over the other man whose breath sounded rasping and strained. Suddenly there was a strange gurgling noise which seemed to fill the street for a few seconds. Candice stiffened, listening, watching - wondering. Then there was nothing except the laboured breathing of the tall man echoing in the cold blackness.

Shocked Candice shrank back from the window as the tall man stood up and moved towards the parked car. He seemed to stagger and when he came into the lamp-light, his face was clearly visible. Candice stuffed her fist into her mouth as she almost cried out in surprise. It was Ollie, she was sure of that, but what was he doing here - fighting? The Ollie she knew wouldn't hurt a fly let alone brawl in the street. The car didn't look familiar and for a second doubt flitted through her mind, but as he walked to the car she recognised his gait even though he was obviously winded and not fully upright.

She wanted to call out to him but for some reason she couldn't; her voice wouldn't come. Candice watched him with a growing feeling of dread. He opened the car door and fell into the driver's seat. Fascinated, confused, terrified, her body was rooted to the spot, all but paralysed. Then all she could think about was Ollie - he was injured she was sure. He needed her.

Candice raced downstairs and fiddled with the lock and chain determined to get to him, to help him. She heard the car start just as she got the front door open. She managed to glimpse a white-faced Ollie hunched over the steering wheel as he drove off, wheels screeching as he tried to right the car which almost hit the curb opposite. Candice yelled after him but he hadn't even seen her, let alone heard her. The car sped off into the distance filling the chilled atmosphere with exhaust fumes.

Chapter Five

Remembering the other man she looked over at the prone figure lying on the pavement. Terrified at what she might find she approached the still figure cautiously.

'Hello, can you hear me?' she whispered, peering at him. 'Are you all right?' She edged closer. There was no answer, just the rustle of the trees and leaves in the hedges.

'Are you hurt? she tried again moving closer still. 'I saw you fighting.' No response. The figure was a silent heap on the pavement. Fear gripped Candice. What had Ollie done? The man's face appeared deathly white in the light of the street lamp. His eyes were half open but they didn't respond to her when she leaned close to him.

'Shall I call an ambulance?' she ventured. At a loss what to do she was loath to touch him or leave him to get help. She'd left her mobile by her bed anyway, she remembered. Bending so her ear was in front of his mouth she struggled to hear if he was breathing, her heart pounded so loudly. The frightened woman placed her hand on his open lips but she wasn't sure if she could feel any breath or not.

Glancing up and down the street she looked for a sign of life, someone to help her but all the houses were in darkness, there just wasn't anyone else around. There wasn't any option, she'd have to scream for help.

Just as Candice opened her mouth a car came hurtling down the road. Thank God, she thought, waving her arms wildly hoping the driver wouldn't drive straight on mistaking her for one of the scammers everyone was being told to watch out for. The ones where a faked road accident got drivers to stop so they could be mugged and their cars stolen.

The car started to weave across the road erratically and she tried to run along the pavement to catch driver's eye waving her arms and shouting. She couldn't see the driver, it was moving too fast, at the wrong angle. Suddenly the car swerved and came right at her. She froze for a split second, confused, wondering what to do. Too late her brain sprang into action warning her to move, to get out of the way. The car was making right for her. There wasn't time. There wasn't time except to glimpse the white-faced person hunched over the steering wheel, aiming right for her.

*****

76

As the car ran over her and she fell to the pavement beside the prone body of the unknown man Candice didn't scream. Her last thoughts were of Ollie. Why?

The car jerked to a stop and the engine ticked in the silence that followed. After a while the driver's door opened and a doubled-over figure gradually eased himself out and made his way around the car to the girl in the dressing gown partially pinned under his front wheels. He shook from head to foot and tears streamed down his stricken face as he realised who it was.

'Candice! Candice! No! Please! No!' His voice rose in a wail as he bent over his former lover.

'What have I done? Oh God! Candice, Candice answer me, are you all right?' He tried to wipe his tears away to see her face better but they gushed down his face. 'Please, please be all right.'

Blood pooled where she lay as he reached to hold her in his arms. He couldn't work out where it was coming from as he tried to check her upper body - her middle and legs were pinned under the car. He dare not try to move it. Then he saw it was coming from the man lying near her. The knife still sticking in his guts. Pain overwhelmed Ollie and he blacked out for a few moments. He came round wondering where he was for a fraction of a second, then he remembered Candice, the man, the knife, the accident. He felt so tired, his body felt cold, he wanted to sleep but he knew he had to get help.

Ollie reached inside his jacket, found his pocket and felt for his phone. It slipped from his grasp and for a moment he wondered why, then remembered he had been stabbed in the chest - the reason why he was finding it harder and harder to breathe. Foamy blood began to trickle down his chin and he coughed. Ollie watched the red spray hit the pavement next to him. Fascinated, he realised he had little time.

'Operator, which service please?' His emergency call was answered almost immediately.

'Ambulance and police – please be quick, I've little time.' He coughed up more blood, his breathing shallower and with his vision fading he focused as best he could on the reassuring voice.

Ollie spoke to the operator for a little longer answering her questions, giving her information. He needed to explain, to tell his story before it was too late. He was reassured that the conversation was being recorded - routine these days.

Three minutes later the ambulance and police arrived to find three bodies lying on the pavement. All were pronounced dead at the scene.

Chapter Six

After an initial investigation the team of detectives decided that they had all the facts, what little there were. Ollie had given a statement to the 999 operator – all recorded – explaining that he and his girlfriend had split up twelve months earlier, after five years together. He had wanted to visit her and try for a reconciliation – his voice on the tape sounded weak and at times he mumbled, but they could understand enough to get the gist of what had happened.

Ollie explained he'd confided in a work colleague, asking his opinion and advice. He told the operator he was stunned when his colleague - someone he regarded as a friend - told him that a reconciliation was out of the question; Candice and he were now lovers.

'How long has this been going on?' Ollie had asked his friend. His voice faltering as he relayed the conversation.

'Actually, on and off for a few years.' His so-called friend had informed him. 'That's why she chose me in the end, dumping you.'

Ollie was stunned – he told the operator – and couldn't take it in, but it all made sense; the arguments, the eventual break-up. He'd always felt she'd manoeuvred things so they'd row and she'd have an excuse to end things. Her new lover seemed to revel in telling him details of their meetings, their time together, and how they fooled Ollie for so long.

However, the more salacious the story became - Ollie told the operator - the more he started to wonder; to have doubts. He wanted proof. He wanted to know for himself. Candice he knew, would never see him or answer his calls.

The last time he'd spoken with her, just after they'd separated, he'd asked her, 'is there someone else? Tell me there is and I won't hold out hope.' She had slammed the phone down without a word.

Ollie told the operator that's when decided to spy on her. Driving past her house on the nights he was told Candice would be entertaining his colleague. Several times he'd pass by slowly looking for a hint, a sign they were in there together. But he'd not seen anything to confirm his colleague's claims. No car outside, no signs of life other than a glimpse of Candice now and again - always alone. Ollie started to have doubts about his former friend's revelations but, hedging his bets, he decided to follow him too, and see where he went. Perhaps they met elsewhere.

It soon became apparent that Candice wasn't visiting or entertaining his former friend or anyone else for that matter. Ollie discovered his friend and colleague was watching her; secretly.

'This evening I followed him again and watched him hide in the bushes opposite Candice's house for the third night running. Every time I drove past he was there in the bushes, hiding, watching her. Several times I saw him in the rear view mirror as I passed. I felt afraid for her,' Ollie told the operator as his breathing deteriorated and coughing spasms took hold more often.

'I lost the plot and wanted to have it out with him, so I parked the car and confronted him on the pavement across from the house. It got violent, we struggled and he pulled a knife on me.' More coughing was audible on the tape. Time was running out it was obvious.

The operator waited for the coughing to stop and encouraged Ollie to carry on – the longer she kept him talking the more chance he had of survival, she thought.

'I felt a searing pain in my chest and I knew he had stabbed me. We wrestled some more and the knife was between us, he held on to it and somehow - as God's my witness - somehow he sort of fell on it.' Ollie's voice broke and the operator waited whilst he coughed.

'Go on,' she said, 'the ambulance is just down the road, try to hang on a bit longer.'

'I know I'm dying, it doesn't matter. Candice, Candice is dead.'

He was silent for a long time and the operator thought he'd died, but then he began talking again.

Ollie explained that he had got back into his car to try to get to the hospital, he knew he had to get medical attention for himself. His former friend was beyond help. When he got to the end of the road he suddenly felt really ill, his vision was blurring, the pain in his chest was unbearable and he almost blacked out at the wheel, so he decided to go back to the scene of the accident and ring for help. Hoping someone had heard the commotion and would come to their aid.

He didn't see Candice as he drove back. He'd blacked out behind the wheel and the next thing he knew the car had stopped. He got out and there she was, pinned under his wheels. Dead. Instead of watching over her, protecting her, he had killed her.

*****

Epilogue:

The Police closed the case regarding the death of both men and no further action was necessary. They concluded, following post-mortems on both men, that Ollie had died as a result of a wound to the heart inflicted by his colleague, Michael Dewar, who had himself died of a stomach wound, which he himself had caused.

The forensic pathologist had never seen the like before. Ollie had taken longer to die but he was indeed killed by the man who died before him. The knife was proven to have been owned by Dewar and Ollie's story was confirmed by the police's forensic investigation.

They checked Dewar's phone records and discovered he had been calling Candice for over two months but she had never returned the calls. Dewar had detailed notes about Candice in his diary which they found when they searched his flat, going back almost a year covering when and where he had watched her. Her whole life was recorded: even what she wore and where she shopped. There was enough information about Candice for the police to conclude he had been terrorising her and planned to kidnap her eventually. His fixation and obsession with her had intensified over the period of a year starting with him watching her every move, and climaxing with his possession of a knife with the intention to kidnap and most likely kill her the evening he died.

From his dying statement to the emergency operator the police concluded that Ollie had accidentally killed his ex-lover whilst trying to return to the scene of the accident, when he was temporarily incapacitated as a result of his fatal wounding; case closed – no further action.

THE HONEY TRAP

They flirted in the bar, drinking and chatting until the music stopped and the bartender shook his head. No more drinks.

Taking the hint they moved towards the revolving doors about to make for the bright city lights and another hotel bar when his young companion shook her head and whispered her suggestion. Why not go upstairs to her friend's room and have some more drinks? Luckily her friend was away for the night and she had the key - what did he think?

He thought it was a great idea. She thought he was too drunk to travel much further anyway and the prospect of getting the almond-eyed beauty into bed was more than he could resist, she was sure. He nodded and followed her to the elevator.

She pressed the button for the tenth floor, snuggling up to him, nibbling his ear, whispering suggestive things in a husky voice full of promise. She knew he couldn't believe his luck.

His meeting with the Ministry of Trade representatives had gone well and they'd decided to go for dinner at the Majestic Hotel a few blocks away. At dinner he and his colleagues were introduced to several young ladies, beautiful, and fluent in English. A little reward for getting the Eastern Europeans to sign the contracts with the minimum of hassle, they'd all assumed.

She had made it clear that she fancied him from the start and they were soon alone, the others having returned to their hotels with companions of their own no doubt. He had hoped she would want to spend the night with him, it had been on his mind all evening.

They reached her friend's room, she opened the door and put the light on, kicking off her stilettos and heading for the hotel fridge as he put the 'Do Not Disturb' sign on the door. He took his jacket off, placing his over-sized briefcase on the floor near the bed.

He moved behind her, kissed her neck and her smooth soft brown shoulders, taking in her musky scent as he ran his hands over her hips and thighs. She turned to kiss him and soon they were heading towards the bed.

Before things went any further she smiled slyly and headed for the bathroom. He understood. Quickly and silently he moved around the room checking the drawers, the cupboards, and looking under the bed and behind the pictures and lamp fittings. The Cold War might be over, he thought, but he knew a Honey Trap when he saw one. Surprisingly he found nothing, which worried him more than if he had found a hidden camera and microphone. His brand new clothes folded neatly and now covered in plastic, were placed in his over-sized briefcase before he got into bed, naked.

After quite some time she returned, perfumed, teeth cleaned, all smiles and full of enthusiasm. Before long they were having sex which - although he was enjoying himself as much as his partner appeared to be - didn't stop him from keeping one eye on the bedroom door. He was sure that her controllers would be rushing in before long, ready for the *blackmail pitch*. Therefore he had to work fast.

He turned her onto her stomach and she squealed with anticipation. Running his hands over her back and shoulders he leaned towards her and nuzzled her neck. She lifted her head to meet his lips as he quickly took the scarf he had hidden under the pillows and expertly wrapped it around her neck. At first she seemed surprised and then, thinking it was all part of the game, smiled wantonly at him. After all, it was her job to please him.

Suddenly he began to squeeze tighter and tighter. Somewhere in her oxygen-starved brain, as she began to choke, it dawned on her that this wasn't a game after all. By then it was too late. The last thing she saw was his laughing face gazing at her as she died.

He rose and dressed in an all-in-one hooded forensic suit which he removed from the over-sized briefcase, where it had been sealed in plastic, before quickly pulling on surgical gloves. Expertly he placed her body on the plastic sheet he'd spread over the floor. He removed the sheets and pillowcases from the bed, folding them neatly before covering them in plastic bags and placing them in his large briefcase along with the wine glass he'd used. He took her plastic-wrapped body into the bathroom, unrolling her into the bath where he washed her body and her hair.

After she was dry he took her back into the bedroom and laid her on the stripped bed, arranging her in his favourite pose.

He cleaned the bathroom quickly and expertly. The plastic sheet and forensic suit returned to his bulging briefcase, he changed back into his clothes and with a last glance round the hotel room - checking he had left no trace of presence - he silently let himself out of the room and made his way down the back stairs to the deserted alley where his driver waited for him.

He felt a sense of relief and elation as they drove away, sure in the knowledge that this was another 'situation' which would go unreported by the authorities. After all, she was their agent and her job had been to involve him, the Second Secretary at the British Embassy, in what has always been known as *'A Honey Trap,'* so they could blackmail him into working for them. Well, he was too good for them, he thought, as he settled back in his seat.

He had been in his position for years working all around the world, allowing himself to be drawn into their so-called *'delicate situations,'* and yet he had never been caught. He enjoyed his work and loved to tease the enemy. He knew his little calling card would be recognised but what could they do? Admit they had planned to compromise a British diplomat who just happened to eliminate their *'Honeybee'* before they could act? He didn't think so.

Next month he was being posted to Tel Aviv. He heard the women there were beautiful and knew how to handle themselves. They all had to do a stint in the Army. The challenge thrilled him. He couldn't wait.

THE LOOK

Chapter One

The first time he saw her photograph he knew she was the one. His heart nearly exploded with excitement gazing at the pretty blonde with huge blue eyes and full lips staring invitingly at him. *She had the look.*

He smiled as he clicked *Accept Friend Request.* He just knew she'd send a request. Their relationship had blossomed during several exchanges on the open group *Photographs and History* forum where they both had expressed the same likes and dislikes.

Waiting for her next message he thought about it. How he would do it, where he would do it. When he would do it. They all made it so easy, he chuckled to himself, as he imagined it. They were going to meet in real life.

They went into *Chat* discussing locations worth shooting in their area and agreed to meet Saturday lunch-time in the *Frog and Wicket* on the river bank, have a drink together and then spend the afternoon taking photos of the mill which was a local beauty spot. The pub was always crowded and it was easy to go unnoticed, he thought, picturing events.

She smiled to herself as she typed, thinking about him, meeting him, photographing him, watching his brown eyes when - she shivered at the thought. *He had the look.*

*****

The pub was heaving with locals but they managed to get a table. He had Glenmorangie on the rocks, she had a Virgin Mary. He smiled as he watched her watching him. She smiled a secret smile back. He thought it was going to be a push-over. They discussed photography and cameras and what they liked to photograph the most. Both loved locations and moving water it transpired.

'Let's go,' he said, draining his glass. Licking his lips he stood and waited for her, managing to secret the glass inside his jacket pocket. She looked so much better in the flesh. He could hardly wait. 'The light is just great today.'

'Can't wait,' she answered, getting the measure of him. She moved from behind the table glancing around, checking that no-one was taking any notice of them. The blonde followed him outside, keeping some distance between them as they walked towards the river and out of sight of the pub. 'It's lovely here.'

It was a gloriously sunny day with a gentle breeze and the only noise apart from the wildlife was the sound of water as it slid over the algae covered water mill paddles.

They were alone apart from the swans and ducks pecking at the edge of the river bank.

Such a perfect spot she thought.

Such an ideal place he thought.

Chapter Two

For the next couple of hours they photographed the mill, the river, and surrounding area, chatting about the history of the place and the right angles and light to get the best shots. All the time he watched her, waiting for the right moment to make his move. Luckily very few people had ventured their way and so he knew they wouldn't disturbed once he decided.

She studied him from beneath her lashes, noting his powerful shoulders, his dark hair, and especially his body language. She waited for him to make his move. Her pulse steady. It would be soon.

'Let's take a break.' She sat on a low stone wall by the water wheel and stretched her long shapely legs, gazing up at him, smiling. 'It is perfect here.' The water rushing behind them the only sound as the mill paddles moved gently through the water.

'Yeah, that would be nice,' he agreed, sitting next to her, close enough to smell her perfume. He could even feel the heat of her leg against his. They checked through the photos they had taken, deleting some, saving others, and as they chatted he kept a discreet look out for passers-by.

He removed his jacket and put it on the wall beside her as he watched some swans taking off from the river. Watching him she carefully felt for the glass he had stolen, unaware she'd noticed. He didn't see her remove the glass and place it in her own pocket.

As he bent to pick his camera case up she bent to help him, brushing against him as she scanned the area quickly. They were alone. She leaned against the wall seductively and waited.

His eyes burned bright, she could feel his tension.

'You look lovely, hold it while I take your photo.' He pointed his Canon at her and took several rapid shots. She smiled and posed, all the time poised, ready.

'Let me take some of you now.' She gestured towards the wall so he had his back to it and the river. 'Put your camera down, I don't want that in the shot,' she added with a sly smile.

'Give me your profile.' He turned away from her and she moved closer faking her shots. 'Now turn to face the river, the light is great now and I want to see if I can get your outline against it, like a silhouette.' He turned his back and waited.

A quick look round then, sure they were unobserved, she shoved him hard in the back. As he toppled over the wall her camera clicked rapidly capturing him as he hit the water and disappeared beneath the huge slow-moving paddles which barely registered his passing.

She watched for a few moments making sure he wasn't going to reappear and then she collected his camera, deleted all the photos, and removed the memory card. Checking to see if anyone was around she wiped the camera with the large cloth she had in her bag and, sure that there weren't any prints on it, hurled it into the fast running water wrapped in his jacket which she'd searched thoroughly. She took the glass from her pocket and wiped that clean as well, wrapping it in the cloth she had been given years ago and had never used, she smashed it against the wall.

When she was satisfied it was in small enough pieces she emptied the cloth into the water below and threw the cloth in after. It floated under the paddles and disappeared.

Chapter Three

Her mobile to her ear she waited for her call to go through as she walked confidently towards the village car park. The pub was still overflowing and the noise was deafening. She would be glad to get back home to Monaco - England had lost its appeal.

'Hey, just to let you know I've sorted the problem,' she said as she got into her hire car.

'Are you sure? the girl replied, her voice shaking.

'Yep, all done and dusted. Call the others and let them know.' She placed her camera on the back seat whilst she removed her blonde wig and blue contact lenses. She would dispose of them later, along with his memory card.

'I'll get the *Photographs and History* group taken down.'

'Yeah, I'm sure. Take it down right away. He won't be social networking or raping anyone else ever again.' She put her phone on hands-free and reversed the car out of the car park and headed towards the main road.

'I'll be in touch in a few days but in the meantime check the email account we set up. I'm sending photos. When you have all seen them, delete them and delete the account. Never use it again and do not keep copies.' She waited to join the motorway.

'OK we will, we know what to do. Thanks.' The girl sat on her bed with shaking knees. 'The money will be in your off-shore account as soon as we've seen the photos and proof he has gone. And then it is over, really over.'

'I will send a text, not from this phone, to say the money has been received and then I shall delete your number and get rid of both phones. You must delete my number and change your phone as well. Understood?'

'Yes, yes, thanks, from all of us, we can't thank you enough.' The girl was almost choking. 'He had to be stopped, the police couldn't catch him and he would have gone on and on and...' she began sobbing.

'Well, he has gone and it is over so do as I say and then forget me and him and move on with your life; all of you, move on.' She hung up the phone.

*****

Back in Monaco she checked her bank account and made the call. She had kept an eye on the news and internet but had not seen anything about a missing man fitting her 'assignment's' description, so she assumed that he had covered his own tracks so successfully he was able to disappear without being missed. That suited her fine.

The phone rang and she glanced at the screen before accepting the call. It came from her contact; the person who found her assignments for her and made all the arrangements.

She smiled as she listened to her next assignment and she rummaged in her desk for paper and pen. She took the details down asking a few questions before hanging up.

She glanced at the information, memorising it, and she burned the paper as usual. Tomorrow she had to do some research into Investment Bankers and Insurance companies. Her new assignment was going to be tough, worth more money than her last assignment which, she acknowledged, she would have done for nothing given the low-life she had dealt with. But this new assignment was high profile and the risks enormous, even dangerous for her, and she had a lot of planning to do before she could begin.

She would be away from her lovely villa for some time to come and she sighed, thinking about the months ahead, living a new life in a new country biding her time until she could carry out her work.

This one would be the last, she mused, as she poured herself a glass of Cristal. This one will bring in enough to last a lifetime, even with my excesses, she thought. She smiled to herself and toasted her contact and her future as she gazed at herself in the mirror.

She liked what she saw. She would fit her new role; she had *The Look*.

UNDERCOVER

A short extract from Ms Birdsong Investigates...

For the last three years she had lived another life, had buried her real self taking on the mantle of a hardened Madam - a trafficker of girls, the worst kind of criminal - and, for the umpteenth time she had fought nausea as she negotiated with the Eastern European.

Her control back at command had shown concern the last time they'd met. She could see the physical and mental toll this assignment was having on her but they were committed now; there was no going back. The team had spent too long infiltrating the organisation and she was their only hope. During the time she had been undercover she had alerted them to more shipments of girls than she cared to recall, but the risk had grown with her every betrayal.

She knew it was only a matter of time before they rumbled her and her life wouldn't be worth a fig if the team were unable to protect her and extradite her at exactly the right moment. The latest shipment had arrived at Heathrow only hours before and were already on their way to a secret location in Oxfordshire where there would be an auction of the girls, some as young as eight, and where the special unit of police would be waiting to raid them. Her message had been received and the team was ready for any trouble which might ensue.

Marko eyed her from the bed as she gathered her clothes and prepared to shower and dress. He didn't trust her any more, she seemed nervous and remote these days and his gut didn't feel right; she didn't feel right. For a long time he'd had suspicions. She seemed to be softening towards the girls under her control and he was debating whether to remove her from her role as Madam of the main whore house which she'd run so successfully. Too many things had been going wrong lately. Too many shipments had been discovered and although he had managed to remain more or less anonymous and untouchable, he knew his luck would run out unless he acted soon. Was it her? He hoped it wasn't but he would soon know; the trap was set. If the latest consignment of girls was discovered and raided, he would know.

She lingered in the bathroom, fully dressed, senses heightened. Marko had been a bit distant and had appeared suspicious of her movements all week. He seemed to make a point of repeating the instructions for the latest intake of girls - where they would be - even giving her more detail than usual about on-line bidders. Something wasn't right. She needed to contact control. Marko's kiss goodbye seemed final somehow when she left his room.

As she pulled to door gently towards her, the phone rang inside. She hesitated, listening to the conversation, her ear against the door; terror gripped her as she heard his words. She turned. A strong pair of arms grabbed her and a gloved hand clamped over her mouth as she screamed….

This story is to be continued….I hope you've enjoyed this little taster from Ms Birdsong Investigates Murder in Ampney Parva…first in my crime/thriller series of novels - which is almost completed – about a Former MI5 Officer, Lavinia Birdsong.

See my social media pages for updates and drop in to say hello sometime.

Thanks for reading my short stories. Another collection will follow in the near future.

Jane Risdon

Made in the USA
Monee, IL
29 December 2021

87519943R00062